L ROSE

PROTECTED

BY THE BEAR SHIFTER

First edition
ISBN: 9780645932850

TRIGGER WARNING

Murder, violence, crime, hate slurs, sexual content, blood, homophobia.

BLURB

Deacon

From the outside, people see me as a businessman who lives with his two brothers and likes to keep to himself. However, the inside is something else. I share my soul with a beast of a bear, and all he knows and wants is to torture and kill.
Until we scent *him*.
Our *fated* mate.

Rio

My life has never been my own. My ruthless father and mess of a mother control it. All I want is to spend my days without looking over my shoulder and without the fear of getting so close to someone that my crime-boss father will use them against me.
At twenty-two, I'm tired, unloved, and live a dull, empty existence.
Until *he* walks into my world—all intense eyes and broody growls that don't sound human.
Now, there's no going back. Not when my soul recognizes his. All that's left to decide is how far am I willing to go to escape my toxic family so I can start anew with the man who makes me feel more in a matter of moments than I have in my whole life.

For my readers who like a growly bear shifter that's slightly unhinged.

CHAPTER ONE

DEACON

Leaning back on the couch, I ignored my inner beast snarling for this man's blood and smirked at the short, old, and balding psychiatrist who sat across from me.

He cleared his throat and straightened on his seat. "So, Mr. Blackwood, what brings you into my office?"

His muddy brown gaze glanced up and quickly back down to the clipboard in his hand. It held the form I'd filled in earlier for this new appointment.

My bear rumbled inside of me as the man's unease slid into my senses, making me want to hold my nose. He reeked, of not only that, but mistrust and a bit of fear.

The only scent that we craved was fear because we thrived from it.

1

"It's all written there, Doc." I tipped my chin at the form.

"Yes, well, I'd still like for you to tell me." He tucked his pen behind his ear and scratched at his chubby cheek while he glanced at the clock on the wall.

"My brothers are annoying me," I told him, stretching my arms along the back of the couch, which I sat in the middle of. My suit jacket pulled open, and I caught him glancing at my sides.

Was he looking for a gun?

Amusement swept through me, tugging up the corner of my mouth. I didn't need a weapon. Not when I was one. Though, my brothers preferred them.

"How so?" he asked, wiping at the sweat forming on his brow.

"They're younger," I simply said, kicking my feet up on the coffee table between us.

He hummed under his breath. "Mr. Blackwood, if you're not willing to elaborate without my prompting, I'm not sure I'm going to be the right therapist for you." He didn't even look at me when he spoke.

I cocked my head to the side. "Is this something you say to all your new patients?"

He cleared his throat, adjusting his position again. "Ah, well...." The soon-to-be dead man finally looked at me again when I placed my feet on the floor and leaned forward to rest my elbows on my thighs, clasping my hands in front of me.

His throat slowly moved over a hard swallow.

"Now, about my brothers. You see, they're a little

insane. Honestly, me included." His brows shot up. I grunted. "Though, it's understandable with what happened in our upbringing. It's what drew us together, connected us. Well, besides our foster mother. We're not even blood brothers, but we bonded like them, because of the savage way our families ripped into us for being the weakest in our homes. In the end, we became one fucked-up family since our packs didn't even help us after we'd gone feral."

"Feral? Insane?"

I nodded. "We went a little crazy for blood and violence for a while."

He stared at me, features schooled to a neutral look, but I could see his thoughts running in his eyes.

Is this guy really insane? Do I need help? Do I call for help?

"Packs?"

Rolling my eyes, I chuckled. "That's what you focus on now?"

He shifted slightly as his heart rate increased, making him stink even worse. "O-Okay then. Ah, what do you mean? What are you talking about being feral and hungry for... blood? And humans? Like you're not, ah, one?"

I waved his questions away. "Doesn't matter. Let's get back to me venting about my younger brothers."

"N-No, please. I'd like to know what you mean about being feral." He cleared his throat and flicked his gaze all around me, but not on me. "You... you also said packs, like it's used for animals. Do you class yourself and your brothers as animals?" He swiped at his sweaty upper lip.

Obviously, he was still trying to reach for a human explanation for my words.

A vindictive smile emerged on my lips. "In fact, Doc, we do."

He nodded over and over to himself as he relaxed a little. He probably thought I was using metaphors when it came to being feral animals.

He'd soon discover he was wrong.

He hummed. "I'm sorry, but I'm doubting your statement since an animal wouldn't dress or speak as you do." He forced a chuckle. "So, please tell me why you would call yourselves animals?" He started tapping his pen to the clipboard. "Do you mean through work? What do you do?"

Smirking, I leaned back into the couch once again, resting one arm up along the back. "You've got it all wrong, Doc. We really are beasts, but at least I like being an animal. I enjoy the violence, the blood, the hunt. It means I can deal with vile, dirty creatures... like you are."

Instantly, color drained from his face and his wide eyes slowly climbed up to mine. He flinched from my hardened gaze. "W-What?" The clipboard slipped from his loose hand and dropped to the ground.

Terror saturated the room, and I drew it in with a big breath.

My smile grew while my bear rumbled inside me. He pushed against my leash, wanting out to devour the abhorrent thing before us, but my bear would never be free unless *I* allowed it.

"I've heard a lot about you, Doc. How your sessions

with your younger patients become hands-on." My upper lip rose in a silent snarl.

"N-No, you're wrong. I would never—"

"Lies," I roared, my beast rattling my chest.

Urine filled the air.

"Fucking disgusting. You pissing yourself only adds to your guilt. You wouldn't be so scared otherwise. Besides, I wouldn't be here if it wasn't true, if I hadn't already seen the proof, you sick fuck."

He went to stand but collapsed back into his seat, muttering, "T-There's no proof. I didn't—"

"Don't," I warned roughly.

He froze while I slowly stood.

"There's no use trying to talk yourself out of it. The end will be the same." I kicked the coffee table out of the way, and he let out a whimper, body trembling. "With you dead." Holding up my hand, I watched his eyes as tears formed and fell when my nails elongated and sharpened right in front of him.

Annoyance rolled through me when he started sobbing. I should have guessed he'd be a crier. Begging would come next. But before he could open his mouth to utter a word or scream, I lunged and slashed my claws across his jugular.

Blood sprayed, hitting me in the face.

"Fucking hell," I muttered while the doc gripped his throat and choked on his blood.

Moving over, I grabbed the coffee table and straightened it, planting the wood in front of him. I sat on it and watched as his life slowly leaked out of him. When I let my bear shine through my gaze and my canine teeth lengthened in a partial shift, a snort of humor escaped me as the sick fuck tried to scream, but it came out as a gurgle.

I should have filmed this for my brothers.

After a low rumble from my bear, the fucker slumped lifeless into his chair.

My phone vibrated inside my pocket. I pulled it free and saw my brother's name on the screen. "Nox?"

"You done? We've got that other meet in an hour."

Shit. "I've got to clean up, and then I'll be ready."

"Good because you know what'll happen if I have to deal with this dickhead."

I did.

Nox wasn't a patient shifter. He took what he wanted, but when it came to the cartel, we had to tread a little more carefully since there were thousands of them. Not that my group couldn't handle them if we had to. We would and in the end, we'd be the victors. But I didn't want to deal with Nox and our other brother, Riker, complaining about all the injuries we'd no doubt get and then heal from. Also, we had a few hired humans help us, who we had to take care of.

"I said I'd be there, and I will."

"Fine," Nox stated and hung up. Riker must have pissed him off; usually he wasn't so surly.

Okay, that was a damn lie. He was always a grump, but with me, he tried to curb it—one of the benefits of my bear being more alpha than his tiger and he didn't want to irk my beast. The last time that happened, we fought, and he ended up with two broken legs. Then again, I didn't leave Nox alone with Riker too much because our brother, in his human or fox form, could annoy the calmest of men with his hyper personality.

Pocketing my phone, I sighed down at the mess.

This was the worst part of dealing out the punishment, but I wouldn't have anyone else do it. Killing disgusting humans like this calmed our animals in ways nothing else could, and that made the world safer for everyone.

AFTER STEPPING out of my car freshly showered, Riker skipped up to my side from where he'd been leaning against the wall with Nox. "Deacon, I wanna know if we can take this place? I want it. Smells yum and look how busy it is. We'd make millions."

I placed my hand on his shoulder, and he settled for a moment. Looking up at me, he met my gaze instead of his bouncing all around us. "We already have millions, Riker."

"It ain't about the money," he reminded himself.

"Exactly."

He pouted, cocking his head to the side. "Still, it would have been good to add a restaurant to the list of businesses."

"Maybe another time." I dropped my hand and stepped up to Nox. "How many?"

He'd been the one to scout this place before I arrived.

"Twenty inside. Fifteen posing as customers, the other

five in the private room with Santiago. Ten more out back, and we're currently being watched by another six."

Riker snorted and danced around me to the other side while stretching his arms out in front of himself. He always moved nonstop, making most onlookers believe he was on something or drunk. To Nox and me, he was just cunning and smart, but a little different; the torture he'd endured by his old pack had been even worse than what Nox and I had experienced.

"There's another two out there. So, eight. Watching. Waiting." He nodded with a crooked smile.

I believed him, and even though Nox's jaw clenched in irritation for missing the other two, he had faith in his brother. Riker's nose was never wrong.

"Right. Let's get this over with." I started for the door with them at my back.

We didn't expect an attack. Luis Santiago, who was the head of the cartel in this area, was curious to know why we'd asked to meet with him. He also wouldn't have accepted if he hadn't heard of us already. He would have seen the cover story we'd painted decades ago of successful businessmen.

What he didn't know, like most humans, was that shifters were real, and he was about to have three of them on his premises.

As far as I knew, the only humans who knew our true identities were loved ones and trusted friends. Of course, there'd been speculations from randoms—from those who'd seen glimpses and tried to push their thoughts to the world, but not many actually believed them. Besides, it was up to the vampires to take care of and erase all those types of cases.

The only ones, outside of family and friends, who were aware of shifters, vampires, and fae, were a small sect of the government, but my brothers and I had nothing to do with them. The council of our communities placated the government in the know into believing us "others" were harmless.

Another thing the government wouldn't have knowledge of was how our shifter council was responsible for our kill orders—those that would appease our beasts.

We got this job because of our foster mother, Ruth, who was on the council. When she'd taken our younger, feral selves in, she knew what we'd crave in the end. How our beasts hungered for violence in our own twisted way of vengeance. The daily torture routines we'd all suffered at the hands of our families called for an outlet. Not all shifter communities had been like ours: cruel and controlling.

Ruth's wasn't. Thankfully, she'd been patient and kind with us, and understood our need to hurt and kill anyone who targeted those weaker.

Sometimes we wanted the blood of any motherfuckers that pissed us off—we weren't complete angels. Luckily, we knew how to hide our kills, so no one found out.

Pushing the thoughts from my mind, I pulled open the front door and stepped in. The scent of food was stronger inside, making my stomach rumble.

Riker laughed. "See."

"We'll get dinner after," Nox said. That was if things went well and we got what we wanted.

As soon as we reached the front counter, a waitress tucked her shaky hands behind her back and dipped her head. "Welcome. Mr. Santiago is waiting for you."

She walked us through the restaurant, and I could hear her heart pounding in her chest. She had nothing to worry about from us, but I didn't know how Santiago treated his employees.

My brothers and I discretely scanned the guards along the way, using our heightened senses. The hall she took us down to the private function room was quiet, though. Two people moved on their feet at the far end. Other than that, the rest were out in the dining area.

She stopped at a door. "Just in here. The waiter for the room will be along shortly to see if you would like some drinks or food."

With a grunt, I opened the door as soon as she'd started back down the hall. Moving into the room, I made my way over to the table and sat opposite Santiago. My brothers took the chairs on either side of me. At least the seats were comfortable. I rested my hands along the armrests and stared at the man across from us.

His lips twitched. "Mr. Blackwood, welcome. Would you prefer to get down to business, or would you care for some food and beverages first?"

A door opened behind us. I glanced toward Nox and subtlety drew in the scent. Male. Smelled like food and sweat.

"Business," I stated, meeting his gaze once more as I straightened the lapels on my jacket.

Santiago waved the waiter off and I heard the click of the door closing once again. I wanted to sigh when a different door opened in the next second. Instead, I thinned my lips and looked to the younger man that just walked in from the entrance behind Santiago, who was now scowling over his shoulder at the new guy.

"You're late," Santiago clipped.

For a split second, I wanted to rip Santiago's face off and beat it against the wall for his tone against the goddamn stunner of a guy.

The man dipped his head toward his boss, then stood to attention beside the door. Santiago grumbled under his breath about "Ungrateful pieces of shit" as he turned back to me.

It was a struggle to drag my eyes away from the newcomer with his sun-kissed, wavy hair and electric-blue gaze, but I managed to meet Santiago's stare with my own cold one.

Both men and women appealed to me and my brothers, and we'd had our fair share of attraction with all types before leading to a one-night stand. However, with blondie, my reaction was different, instant, and weird. Like I'd never had before. As if an invisible force punched me in the gut to fiddle with my damn organs.

I drew in a breath, but I scented all the other assholes in front of him. They needed to move. I ground my teeth together to stop my bear's grumble.

Yeah, there was something else about him, something *more* than just his looks.

I wasn't sure what exactly, but I'd figure it out.

"Tell me why you wanted this meeting, Blackwood," Santiago ordered.

"We'll pay you a onetime sum of five-point-five

million if you cease importing your products into this area."

Santiago glanced to his main henchman standing to his left before laughing. The monkeys joined in. All except the stunner. Instead, his shock was easily read when he gaped at me like I was an alien.

Until he quickly tensed when he noticed me staring and blanked his expression before looking to the floor. He didn't like that I'd caught his reaction. But did his shock mean that he hoped his boss would accept? Maybe he didn't agree with what went on in the business.

Santiago clicked his fingers and the room quieted.

His cocky smirk had me gripping the armrests of the chair. My bear and I wanted to break every tooth in his too-big mouth and make him eat them; whatever was about to come from his lips, we weren't going to like.

No one else, but me, noticed how my brothers adjusted slightly. Preparing for a fight if it happened.

"I might consider the payment, but not a one-off. I'd request it every year, Blackwood. Honestly, it's hilarious you had the balls to bring this to the table to begin with. Are you stupid?"

"I don't believe so," I said through clenched teeth.

"You have to be." He shook his head and waved around him. "I have an army at my back and all you have are the men sitting next to you and a few hired hands."

Yeah, he'd definitely done his homework on us. But only learning the public knowledge we allowed people to see.

Double-locking my anger and bear down, I replied, "That may be, but I believe it will be in *your* best interest to reconsider. At least think about it longer. We'll be in touch."

Before we could stand and make our exit, the damn door behind us opened again.

The stench of strong alcohol touched my nose just before my attention swung to blondie as he clipped a low, "Shit, Mamá."

CHAPTER TWO

RIO

*S**hit, shit, shit.*

She must have been faking sleep and then followed me. I was sure I'd been carefully quiet. I knew she hated that I still listened to him. But I had no choice. I either worked for *him* or our lives were at stake.

Fuck.

Bile rose, but I swallowed it down and pressed a hand to my gut.

He'd probably kill her for this scene anyway.

"This is where you went," my mamá slurred as she stumbled further into the room.

She waved a hand toward my sperm donor, also known as my father, who I referred—no, I was *trained* to call him by his last name like all his minions did. Mamá laughed humorlessly. "I knew Rio'd be running to you.

14

What do you have him doing now? Haven't you ruined our lives enough?"

"Mamá!" I yelled and started for her. I had to get her out. Could I get her far enough away to hide her?

It's impossible.

No, it wouldn't be. It couldn't be. He wouldn't get her.

Santiago was quickly in my way, grabbing my arm to halt my process.

Shit, fuck, I repeated silently.

This was it. He'd end us.

Mamá stumbled forward, demanding, "You let him go. He's *my* boy. He does what *I* say."

Fear had my heart rabbiting and ears ringing. Paling at the thoughts of what he'd do to us, I tried to pull my arm free. We had to run, to hide.

Christ, Mamá.

Why'd you follow me?

Why'd you come?

Recently, she'd been on my back when I was away from home more and more. What she didn't know was that most of the time I stayed away was simply because I didn't want to be home. I got more studying done at the college library than I did at the house, where she was usually in my ear asking if I was talking to Santiago or if I'd seen him. If not that, she would drunkenly be going on and on about her life with him—before and after it turned to a nightmare.

It was all his fault.

He got her into drugs and alcohol. He screwed around

on her. He flaunted younger flames in front of her and then called her ugly names.

But it was her choice to stick by him for so long. It was *her* choice to sleep with all his men, hoping to make him jealous. It was her choice to let her child be the one to clean up after her on a binge.

Yet I stayed loyal to her and helped as I never wanted to turn out like him.

Santiago tugged me forward until we were nose to nose. "You let that bitch follow you here?"

"I thought she was passed out. I didn't know." I yanked at my arm again, enough that it would leave bruises tomorrow. If I lived until then. "I'll get her home. She won't even remember this."

He studied me with his upper lips raised. Always disgusted by me. "She'd better not, boy, or she won't be the only one dead."

There were sounds of creaking off to the side, but I didn't dare look away from Santiago.

As soon as I nodded, he pushed me aside, hard enough I stumbled back. I quickly twisted and walked to Mamá, who was still ranting loudly in Spanish and waving her arms around.

Walking around the table, near the guests, I noticed the middle one watching my every move with his intense dark brown eyes, while his jaw clenched and nostrils flared. Whatever his problem was, I didn't care. I had my own situation to deal with and it was more important than anything, because the result included my life.

Hastily, I made my way over to the woman who had tried her best at being a good woman and mother when I was younger, before *he* fucked her over after he grew bored of her when I was ten.

She switched to English to say, "I gave you *everything* and you left me, you piece—"

"Mamá," I clipped, stopping at her side. I took her arm gently in hand. Her focus swung to me, and her emotions quickly shut down before a soft smile replaced her viciousness.

"Let's go home," I told her softly and turned us toward the door.

If she was sobering, she usually settled as soon as I was close, and thankfully it was one of those moments.

"Okay, honey," she whispered. Already I could read the shame and worry in her gaze, like every time she'd yell and scream or slap me for looking like him or saying something like him. It only took a thought of that fucker to set her off.

Once outside the doors, Mamá leaned into me. "You lied." Her sniffle cut at my skin. If I followed her instructions and never saw him, we'd be in more trouble, but she didn't understand that. Which was why I'd lied.

No matter what I did, I was screwed.

Not only had he fucked up his ex-wife's life, but my own. I walked on eggshells around both of them. But I could understand Mamá's pain and suffering. If only she'd get help, like I'd asked her to on a number of occasions. Well, I had up until this year, after I turned twenty-two, because I was sick of sounding like a broken record.

Maybe it was time I forced her to go into rehab. Even when I knew that if I took her there, she probably wouldn't speak to me again.

Is that so bad? What does she ever do for me?

Fuck. No. I couldn't think like that. He'd abandoned her. I couldn't do it as well. Even when sometimes I *really* fucking wanted to.

We just needed him out of our lives.

"I did, Mamá. I'm sorry."

"I can't handle you lying, my boy. Not like him."

Clenching my jaw, I nodded stiffly when she glanced up at me.

If he was gone, I wouldn't have to be the middleman. I wouldn't have to lie to her about being around him or have her show up like she did, risking both our lives. If he wasn't around, maybe she'd be happy. And I could be too.

Don't be like him. I'd lost count of the times she'd said those words. Each time it seemed to stoke the fire within from the guilt she lay on me. I wasn't him. I would never be him, and every move I made was to protect our lives.

I'd never be a simple college guy going to parties, staying in a dorm, having fun, getting drunk, or even trusting someone.

My life consisted of studying, cooking, cleaning, and looking after my mother, while trying to do the tasks Santiago asked of me to keep the peace, and so I would never be beaten like I had when I refused that first time.

It wasn't long after I turned twelve when Santiago turned up outside of my school. Before then, he'd left me alone. I'd known he wasn't a man to mess with from what I'd witnessed with how he'd treated Mamá.

I'd had no other option but to get into the limousine with him. The fear had been suffocating when I saw his second-in-charge sitting in the back with him. Half an hour later, after a silent and awkward car ride, we stopped near a bar, but the driver hadn't turned the car off.

"Get out," Santiago had ordered, while he looked down at a folder on his lap. I'd jolted before stilling. I didn't think he was talking to me. The times I had seen him, I was mostly ignored.

His hard gaze moved to me. "Get out."

"Why?" I'd whispered as more fear clogged my throat and I tried very hard not to piss myself.

"You're to go into that bar, ask for Bayden Hiller, and when you find him—" He reached into his pocket and pulled out a folded blade, flicking it open. "—stab him with this while you tell him that I won't wait another week for my money."

As he spoke, my eyes had widened, and I was already shaking my head before he finished his words. Which cost me a backhand to the face.

"No, please—"

He squeezed my cheeks between his thumb and forefinger. "You're my son. You'll do as I say. I let her coddle you for far too long and now look at you. Crying." He'd shoved me back. "Wipe your pathetic face."

I quickly had.

He'd thrust the knife out again, opening his palm. "Take it."

"I-I can't."

Scoffing, he'd turned his nose up at me with a glare before looking to his second and ordering, "Go."

He'd slipped out of the car and was back in moments while I sat there on the verge of vomiting. I'd known something would happen to me for refusing. As his second climbed into the car, I clenched my teeth to stop my gasp at the sight of all the blood. He sat as if it was nothing, and to him it probably wasn't, but I'd never seen so much coating one person's hands.

"Hiller wouldn't have had the money next week either," he told his boss.

Santiago had turned to a new page in his folder. "You took care of it?"

"Yes."

Had that meant Hiller was dead? I'd learned a couple of weeks later, it had. At the time in the car, I'd wanted to ask about witnesses, but I'd been foolish to think anyone would talk against Santiago. No one wanted to face his wrath.

From there, he'd taken my shaking and crying self to his mansion. Then, with the help of his second, Antonio, they dragged me into the basement and beat some sense into me.

However, at the time, he didn't know how stubborn I could be about taking another person's life. Even at twelve, I would rather have died than be forced to kill. I'd silently prayed to God to take care of my mamá, to tell her I was sorry.

Apparently, my stubbornness was a strength he saw in me, and he'd made a deal that if I didn't have to kill anyone, I would become his lackey in other ways. If I agreed, Mamá and I could live, and he'd keep supporting her until I was twenty-three, when I would join the business after I'd finished college.

At twelve, I'd thought it was a good deal. A safe deal. Especially since I thought I was dying anyway after being beaten so bad I couldn't see out of my left eye and my whole body ached. No matter what way I moved, lay, or sat, I'd been in pain for weeks.

So, I'd agreed. And from that day on, he held control over me.

I glanced down at Mamá as I helped her into bed. Why couldn't she have been the one to protect me instead of leaving it up to a little boy? But I knew the answer. She had a weakness for Santiago. A weakness that was a sickness.

My gut twisted from the thought of it.

I'd never fall for someone where I'd just accept everything they did, even if it meant they kept hurting me over and over.

Shaking my head, I glanced at the hallway clock on the way to my room; it was past midnight. I had an early class in the morning. I hoped that whatever Santiago wanted, his business meeting would take priority and he'd forget about me, or he'd at least wait until tomorrow afternoon to contact me again.

If only I didn't have to deal with him.

I'd never wished death on anyone, and I still couldn't, no matter how much he ruined our lives. But I did wish he'd leave us alone. At least he'd kept to his word by never asking me to kill anyone again.

The jobs he did give me were disgusting or boring. Disgusting when I had to clean up after a... disagreement gone wrong or bathrooms at clubs, even though he had many cleaners already on his payroll. And the boring jobs were to watch one of his mistresses. The only task I did like was when he requested my advice for his businesses.

His legal ones. I wasn't privy to the illegal ones until I was completely in the fold at twenty-three.

Where I had to swear my life and loyalty to him and the family. The cartel.

If only I had a choice. If I did, I would move as far away as I could. Unfortunately, his reach meant nowhere would be safe.

It was either sign up for a life of crime, blood, and murder, or die. I didn't want to lose my life, even if it was miserable. One time I tried striking another deal: when I swore my allegiance to the cartel, I could be the behind-the-scenes man. Run the businesses and stay clean. He'd laughed in my face and said that no matter what I did, I'd never be clean. He didn't understand my apprehension over becoming a part of the "family." In his eyes, it was the best way to live. Even told me how I'd be able to get what or who I wanted.

But all I saw was fear and used women.

Everything about the family twisted me up. My skin crawled each time I was near him or his men. I was on damn anxiety meds to help my nerves.

What could I do, though?

There was nothing.

No matter what, I was stuck.

Fuck my life.

Fuck my father.

Fuck everything.

Sighing, I scrubbed a hand over my face and turned on the shower, shoulders dropping from my pitiful thoughts.

When the water was warm enough, I stepped under

the spray and hoped my thoughts would wash down the drain too.

Hope.

Why did I even bother to hope for something else, something more?

Resting my hands on the tiled wall, I once again wished I had a normal life.

Normal?

What even was that?

I didn't know, and I was sure there were many others who were in the same sort of boat. I just wanted to live better days.

Snorting, I grabbed the shampoo and poured some out onto my palm.

Why had Santiago asked me to join him when he was obviously busy in a meeting to begin with? I'd never attended a business deal before. That was if it had been about business. Hell, I couldn't even remember if they spoke before Mamá arrived.

I did recall those intense, fierce eyes. There was something in them that had me thinking—if I had my head together and hadn't been worried about my own situation —I would have done anything to make sure his gaze didn't land on me.

I never wanted to be under his attention again.

CHAPTER THREE

DEACON

*M*ate. *Ours.*

Claim.

As soon as Rio had gotten close to scent, I knew he was mine.

Knowing had my heart frantically drumming while I gripped the armrests to stop myself from pounding my chest and roaring in fucking glee. My bear stood on its hind legs and chuffed contentedly at finally finding our mate.

Christ, I wanted to grin, to damn cheer aloud, but I locked it and my body down so I didn't run after him. I already knew he wouldn't be ready for my world.

The need to tell my brothers and halt this damn meeting had my pulse racing with urgency.

Before Santiago spoke, after my mate and his mother left, I stood. "Give me time to speak with my brothers before we continue." I didn't use pleasantries. I would never beg or plead for anything from this man, and if he didn't give me what I now wanted, then I'd end him in a way that would make his worst nightmare seem like child's play.

Santiago waved me off with a smirk and turned to the man at his side.

When I waited for my brothers to stand, I overheard Santiago whisper, "Have someone keep an eye on my son and his mother. If they try to leave town, bring them in. I'll keep that boy under my thumb one way or another."

His meaning was clear. He would murder his ex to gain more control over my mate.

I wouldn't allow it.

Kill, my bear demanded. Soon we would know if we kill Santiago or if we could gain the upper hand and take control over this piece of shit.

We were willing to take his life if he didn't shut down his business in our area, but I had to find out what Rio thought of his father first before acting on anything.

In the corner of the room, far enough away from human ears, I looked to Riker and Nox.

"His son is my *fated* mate," I stated proudly, but also quiet enough no sound would pick up if we were being filmed. We couldn't hear anything, which was foolish on their side, though there was equipment quiet enough that even our shifter hearing didn't register.

Riker clamped his hand over his mouth. No doubt he

would have yelled in happiness for me. It was easy to read by his bright eyes.

"Are you sure?" Nox asked. He was always the skeptical one.

"Yes. I scented it. I *feel* it, so does my bear. I don't know how I was graced with a fated mate, but they have gifted me something precious. I won't ignore this. He's to be mine."

"There's obstacles," Nox said.

"He might not like guys," Riker added, and then laughed lightly. "To see you chase is gonna be so much fun."

Even Nox smirked at that.

"Shut up," I snarled. "Tonight, we call off the offer and come back at a different time. I need to figure out what Rio thinks of his father and his dealings."

"Rio—" Riker thinned his lips when my bear made an appearance in my glare. "I was going to tell you that you already say his name cute-like."

Closing my eyes, I took a deep breath and opened them again without my bear present.

"Careful, Riker," Nox warned as my upper lip raised.

Riker nodded. Yet the smile never left his face as he moved from one foot to another.

Jesus.

"Let's go," I ordered. We went back over to the table but didn't take our seats. Instead, we stood behind them. "We'd like to give you some time to consider our offer." I placed my hands on the back of the chair in front of me.

Santiago grunted and shook his head. "Why wait? The offer is pathetic. I won't consider it."

The chair creaked under my grip. Santiago glanced down at my hands and up again with lifted brows.

I hadn't wanted to offer something else to appease him for now, but I didn't see another possible course of action since I needed to figure Rio out first. I shouldn't be hasty and kill his father. The last thing I would want his death to cause a problem in our relationship—that was if Rio felt something for him.

A relationship we'd eventually have.

Surely, I could win him over.

Christ. What if I couldn't win him over?

Fuck that. I would. Somehow, I'd find a common ground with Rio, which would give me time to try and woo the hell out of him.

My bear hummed in encouragement. He believed we'd win him over so we could claim him.

Already I looked forward to tasting his scent on my tongue and sliding into his tightness.

Nox nudged his foot against mine.

Fuck.

Fine.

I had to concentrate on this motherfucker.

"Then give us some time to come up with a better offer for you to consider."

Santiago chuckled and rolled his eyes. "All right, I'll play. I look forward to our next meeting, Blackwood."

His men would be watching us more closely now, which was unfortunate. But something we'd easily deal with since we mastered staying under the radar—when we wanted—a long time ago.

With a nod, I stalked from the restaurant with my brothers.

"Home," I barked before making my way to my car.

The whole drive I kept picturing Rio Santiago. How he'd be mine. *My* fated mate. Mine and my bear's to love always. Eventually, he'd come live with me and my brothers. But if they pissed him off, I'd hurt them.

I could already picture him in our home. In the living room sprawled out on the couch with his head on my lap. As he stood in the kitchen laughing at something Riker said while I watched from the table and ignored Nox as he tried to get me to focus on business.

Focusing would be hard for a few decades or possibly forever when I had someone who'd been made just for me to dote on.

My bear chuffed inside at the idea of our mate in our den. We'd make it perfect for him. Anything he wanted, I would get. If he desired all of my belongings gone, I'd do it. He had to be happy so he smiled all the time. I wanted to make him feel safe, content, and loved. I had a hunch that, for him, those emotions were hard to come by when he had to deal with a fuckhead of a father and a drunk for a mother.

Shit. What would happen if he was like his father?

No. I couldn't believe it. He had to be different from Santiago.

I might be a cold-blooded killer, but at least I had morals. Mostly. And I only killed those who deserved it.

When I got to the house, my brothers were already inside. Walking in, I heard Nox in the kitchen tapping away at his computer. Riker was coming downstairs from his room. He'd be in the kitchen shortly as well.

My skin felt tight. Like I wanted to change forms and hunt. My bear longed for me to pursue our mate. My animal didn't understand we had to take it slow, to get to know him. After all, he was human. We couldn't come on too strong. Therefore, it was lucky I had full control over my beast. Yet, admittedly I was struggling as well. My cock hadn't gone down since I'd scented him, and I'd give my left nut to have him here with me.

Scrubbing a hand at the back of my neck, I dropped it to my side and fisted both. Frustration had me stomping louder than normal through the huge fucking house. It took forever to get to the kitchen.

We'd bought this home ten years ago, and if I didn't have a good sense of smell, I'd get lost in the place that holds ten-bedrooms, five-bathrooms, and three living rooms. It wasn't like we used all the rooms. Nox had three bedrooms set up for his computers. One of the living areas was our gym. Another was a theater that we never watched movies in.

Nox and I would have picked differently, but when Riker found it, he'd fallen, and we didn't have the heart to talk him out of it. I would love the house more when Rio lived here with us.

Smiling, I stepped into the kitchen.

"Your turn to cook" was the first thing Nox said.

Groaning, I went over to the refrigerator and opened it. Grabbing out some meat, I turned to the counter that faced Nox at the table. He was in here instead of his offices for two reasons. The first, he wanted to give me information and talk. The second, he wanted food. Shifters loved to eat.

As I gathered the rest of the ingredients for beef patties, I said, "Hit me."

Nox cleared his throat, but before he spoke, Riker skidded around the corner, yelling, "Wait for me. I want to know about my brother-in-law."

Nox rolled his eyes and shook his head, but I also caught the small grin. His expression quickly blanked as he looked back to the screen. "Rio Santiago is a twenty-two-year-old college student studying for a business degree. His mother, Isabella, worked as a waitress at a bar Santiago frequented."

How'd he know so much already? We'd been home five minutes.

"I already knew this because of the background check I did on Santiago. I just never expected his son to be your fated." His jaw clenched and he glanced down to the computer. "Did I say congrats?"

"You didn't but I appreciate the gesture."

"Me too! Congrats from me too. This is fucking exciting. Makes me want to cut someone up. Do we have anyone?" Riker asked as he sat on the table, swinging his legs back and forth.

"Not at the moment," Nox answered. "All our jobs are done, and no one is hassling any of our businesses."

Riker sighed. "Boring. No one at the office getting on your nerves, Nox?"

Nox grunted. "No. Not at the moment, anyway. Besides, I think we'll have our hands full if Santiago doesn't take our deal. Ruth will need to be told about the delay."

Nodding, I rolled the last patty. Ruth would also be interested in the information about me scenting my fated mate. However, I wasn't ready to tell her, knowing she'd be on the next flight to try and help me woo him.

"What college does Rio attend?" I puffed my chest out at saying my mate's name again.

As Nox told me the college, my other annoying brother yelled, "Aww, look he's— Never mind." He smiled as he quickly dropped his gaze.

"Wait until you two find yours," I said gruffly.

"I doubt we will," Riker answered with a pout. Not every shifter would find their fated one in their lifetime. Ruth hadn't in her one hundred years, but she bonded with another shifter she loved, and married him forty years ago.

"I don't want one," Nox clipped.

I held back my snort.

They could both use one.

Someone who balanced us out. At least, that was what had been taught to young shifters back in the day. I was curious to know if they still taught about fated bonds or if they didn't bother since the number of shifters finding their fated had dwindled as years passed.

I didn't know how I was blessed with one, but I wouldn't question Lady Luck. I'd accept the gift given.

Glancing to Nox, I said quietly, "You will. Having a fated mate never crossed my mind until I scented him. Now all I want to do is make sure he's safe, fed, rested, and happy. It's nothing like we've experienced in our attraction to those we fuck." When he looked up, I rubbed at my chest where it fluttered, and added, "The rush of emotions, all the damn good ones, makes this shit worthwhile. I can already understand why fated mates are protected and cherished. It's because they really are something special. Hell, I haven't even spoken with him, but my bear and I already feel content." Shaking my head, I snorted. "I'd give anything to be at his side checking on him, but I know I'll fuck this up if it's rushed. I think. I don't actually know. Still, I don't want either of you to tell Ruth about Rio yet. I'm worried she'll fuck it up, and then I'll hate her for it. You two had better pull your heads in around him too."

Christ.

I had to stop thinking people would screw this up for me.

I'd put it out in the world that they wouldn't. *I* wouldn't.

Everything will go smoothly, and I'll soon be in my mate's presence.

Riker laughed and wiggled on the table. "When it's time, can I tell Mom?"

"We'll see," I said.

"The plan?" Nox asked.

I got a pan out and heated it up with some oil. "Riker, grab me some rolls and butter them." I'd cut some salad shit up in a second. I placed the patties in the heated pan and waited for the sizzle to settle. "The plan is to take the week to get to know Rio and see what his life is like. I have a feeling he and his father aren't on good terms, but we need to confirm it. I'd also like to keep watch on him." His father's words ran through my mind. "Did you hear what Santiago said before I pulled you two for a chat in the corner?"

Riker nodded as he scowled. "He wants his son under his thumb."

"And that your mate and his mother will be watched," Nox added.

"Meaning?"

They both sat straighter and said in unison, "We protect him at all costs."

Christ, pride for my brothers rolled through me.

I nodded once. "Exactly." But they also understood the outcome if a shifter lost their fated.

Before we went insane, we'd destroy the world.

Nox ran a hand over his short light-brown hair. "He has an early class tomorrow. How about we send Riker in and—"

"No. You."

Nox stilled before he clipped, "Me?"

"Yeah, you won't disrupt the class like Riker." Who was currently grinning like a madman as he buttered the last roll and then went to sit back on the table.

Nox groaned. "Fuck. Okay."

"I'll be outside that classroom figuring out a way to approach him. For now, I'll just be happy someone is watching out for him."

I trusted my brothers with my mate completely. They'd take their own lives before harming him or me.

Riker clapped. "This is gonna be awesome."

"Riker, how about you stay—"

His whole attitude changed as he leaped onto the table

on all fours, in a crouched position. "I'm going."

I clenched my jaw. When he got this way, being stubborn, over something he was excited to be a part of, the only way for him to listen and submit was to take him in a fight to prove my dominance. But I wasn't in the mood to fight.

"You'll behave and do as I say, no matter what it is." I didn't state it as a question. It was a demand.

He rested his butt back on his calves and saluted. "You got it, captain."

Grunting, I plated the burgers and prayed Rio liked our sudden appearance in his life. Especially since I had high hopes of staying there forever.

CHAPTER FOUR

RIO

I ended up with only a few hours of sleep, so of course I still felt like a zombie that hadn't eaten in years. Slowly, I dragged my carcass into the lecture hall and took my usual seat toward the back. I only liked sitting near the rear because the professor didn't bother to call on those who were further away. However, I just remembered he was away for a couple of weeks, and we had a substitute.

Damn, I hoped he was like Professor Higgens. Knowing my luck, he wouldn't be.

My phone vibrated in my pocket. I already knew it would be Santiago. Sighing, I pulled it free.

Your mother?

> Doesn't remember anything.

> Good. Make sure she never follows you again. What I called you in for last night can now wait for a later date. I'll be in contact.

And I'm already looking forward to it, dickhead.

> Yes, sir.

I didn't have the courage to add on the middle finger emoji like I wanted to.

Fuck my life.

Rubbing at my eyes, I placed my phone back in my pocket just as the door opened and, crap on a cracker, it was Professor Rhodes. He was a prick of a professor. In the other class I had with him, he always droned on where it was always a risk of falling asleep.

This was going to be a long hour.

The professor looked around the room and paused on someone to my left as his brows dipped. I glanced there and tensed. The guy looked familiar, but I couldn't think from where.

No matter. I quickly averted my eyes from the imposing man who had what seemed like tribal tattoos on the back of his neck that dipped under his shirt. He was built like he could bench press five men without breaking a sweat. If that wasn't enough, his scowl, even with his pretty golden eyes, had fear filling my veins, and it wasn't even aimed at me. The professor wasn't faring well either. Even from this far I could see sweat forming on his shirt. I definitely didn't want that guy's attention on me for any reason at all.

When Rhodes started to speak, his voice sounded a little shaky, but it quickly went away and all too soon his tone got that dull monotone to it. In fear of drifting off, I took out a pencil and my drawing book, then flipped to a new page.

As I tried to concentrate on the lecture, I started drawing random things to keep myself awake. When my hand was moving, it helped me focus a bit more.

But hell, it was hard.

Sometime later, I leaned back and stretched, glancing around to see if anyone was having the same trouble staying awake. My eyes connected with a girl a couple of rows down and to the left. Her cheeks heated before she smiled, waved, and looked to the front again. I'd noticed her watching me a few times before. Would she be like all the other women before her and ask me out or instead want to be friends? It would be good if she stared at me for another reason than wanting a date.

I huffed to myself. Either way, I couldn't take her up on a date or being her friend.

And she wouldn't be the only one I rejected.

It wasn't that I didn't want to have friends or date. I did. And God, did I want to fuck. To have a relationship. To know if I wanted to marry a woman or a man. I liked both—at least I thought I did. It's hard to know for certain when I'd never dated anyone. There had been a confusing moment in high school when I was attracted to one of my male teachers. Only, the thought of being bi went from my mind when I started college, though, and my body didn't react to any other guy.

Yet, if I had friends or went out with someone, they were then at risk of being seen and used by Santiago. I couldn't risk it.

No. I *wouldn't* risk that.

Which left me a lonely life with my hand to get me off and my own company to be friends with.

Shaking my head, I glanced back down at the drawing and paused.

Eyes.

The intense dark gaze I'd seen the night before at the restaurant.

Why did I draw them?

Wait....

Shitting hell motherfucker.

The guy who sat in the lecture theater had been sat next to the intense-eyes guy.

Shit, shit, shit.

What was he doing here?

My gut twisted. Now would be the time to piss myself as fear pressed against my bladder. I clenched my muscles tightly and then my ass when I heard him shifting in his seat.

Were they here to watch me on Santiago's orders?

No, that couldn't be it. The atmosphere in the room had been thick with tension, which had me thinking it had been their first meeting the previous night.

Could they....

He wouldn't be here to kidnap me.

No one would be that stupid.

Then again, if they were, Santiago would be glad to be rid of me. He wouldn't pay a ransom.

Fuck my life. What do I do?

I bobbed my knee up and down as the nerves licked at my skin. My pulse raced its own race while I tried to look unrattled on the outside. Mentally, I cried, screamed, and rocked over and over.

As I dug my teeth into my bottom lip, I contemplated calling Santiago, but quickly wiped that thought away because there'd be no point. He'd simply laugh and tell me I was on my own.

Fuck, fuck, fuck. What to do? What to do?

I could fight. I'd been trained to, but I had a feeling that what I learned would be considered useless when it came to this guy. Especially if the other two were around as well.

Shit. Were they?

If I ran, would they be lurking around a corner to catch me?

Why me? I groaned internally and looked up at the ceiling. Closing my eyes, I took a deep breath and prayed that whatever they wanted wasn't as bad as I was imagining.

Running a hand over my face, I snorted and looked down at the eyes on the page.

Do I even bother trying to pray when it came to these guys?

Probably not.

Christ. Who would look after Mamá? We had no other relations. Except on Santiago's side, but they were all corrupt like he was.

If shit hit the fan, the only thing I wanted was for her to be safe.

A dull ache of worry started in my chest. I didn't expect her to sober up enough to get herself help. I wished she'd change. That Santiago hadn't consumed her life so much where she got lost to the rest. To me.

Fuck. Why was she like that? Why couldn't she be strong for me, her child? Why had it always been me supporting her?

Why, why, why?

Anger thickened my throat. Not only from those thoughts, but for also allowing them to conjure in the first place. Negativity never got me anywhere in the end.

What did get me somewhere?

Nothing.

I was stuck no matter what I did, where I went, or who I had in my life.

I jolted when the professor clapped loudly and called an end to the lecture.

Quickly, I packed up my things while I nearly swallowed my tongue and tried not to pass out. I darted down the stairs, out the door, and rushed to the front entrance so I could hide in the coffee shop close by until my next class. A coffee shop where there would be a lot of people around, so no one could kidnap me.

If that was their plan to begin with.

But if I was wrong, and instead I'd make a dick out of myself by running around the place in a panic, I'd take the gossip that would, no doubt, start. I wasn't stopping for anything, unwilling to risk being caught by them. If that made me a fool, so be it. At least by hiding, I wouldn't scream or piss myself in front of anyone.

A grunt dropped from my mouth as I fell back on my ass from knocking into, what felt like, a brick wall that appeared out of nowhere.

"Oops, that had to hurt. Did it hurt?" The smaller one out of the three last night crouched down next to me. Eyes widening, I fell back to my elbows and opened my mouth to yell for help, but only managed a noise.

When he cocked his head to the side, orange hair slipped to cover his amber-colored eyes before he blew it away and smiled.

"I thought you saw me." The voice was rough and deep. I lifted my gaze up and up to see *him* standing in front of me with his arms crossed over his chest and a frown on his full lips. He reminded me of the guy from that movie I wanted to see. Kraven the Hunter. Except this guy had the darkest brown eyes I'd ever seen and didn't have a beard around his full lips. Even his longer hair, which was half tied up, was similar to that movie character.

Work, brain, work. And explain to me why I'm looking at his lips to begin with.

"I-I'm not worth kidnapping. My father won't care. So, if you're going to kill me, just—"

The smaller one laughed joyfully.

Intense-eyes guy suddenly bent, and in the next second, I was on my feet with his hands dropping away from me to his sides and fisting.

Did he want to hit me?

He looked a bit bigger and stronger than the guy in

class before. Stronger than I was, and a hit from him could kill.

I swallowed thickly and stared up at him.

"We're not here to kidnap or hurt you," he told me.

My heart gave off a funny beat, like it wanted to believe his words, but I couldn't chance being so trusting.

"Deacon," the smaller one said, glancing off in the distance.

"Is there somewhere we can talk?" Deacon asked.

Clearing my throat, I nodded. "The coffee shop?" Dammit, I made it sound like a question. Could they tell they intimidated me? *Probably, you idiot.* I certainly wasn't acting like having them here didn't bother me.

"Good. Lead the way." Deacon jerked his chin to the side.

And have him at my back? I didn't think so.

I pointed to the left. "It's over there."

His lips twitched before he turned and started that way. The smaller guy hummed a tune under his breath and danced beside me as he walked.

Was there something wrong with him?

He glanced at me, winked, and asked, "Are you gay?"

"Riker," Deacon snarled, spinning toward us. I backed up, holding my hands up in front of me.

Riker rolled his eyes, and timidly, which seemed an act, turned to me, kicking at the ground where he stared. "Sorry. You don't have to tell me, and I shouldn't have asked. You'll have to get used to me blurting things out, because sometimes the noggin'"—he tapped at his temple with his knuckles—"lets my mouth run with words before thinking it could be bad." He pinched at his bottom lip to try and hide his smile.

Deacon sighed. "Forgive my brother. Like he said, he doesn't think sometimes."

There was just something about Riker that made it easy to forgive his slipups.

"It's okay."

"He was drawing your eyes in class. I think he's into men." The voice behind me made me jump, scream, and turn around so fast, I lost my footing and was headed toward the ground until Deacon caught me.

"Where the hell did you come from?" I yelled as I straightened and then stepped away from Deacon.

My new classmate glanced at me before he ignored me and looked to Deacon. "He doesn't concentrate in class and nearly fell asleep many times if it wasn't for his drawing of your eyes—"

"They're not his," I claimed loudly, pointing at the man whose eyes I had drawn.

Why was Deacon smiling?

I glared. "They weren't yours," I demanded snappishly, and then added to Riker, "And no, I'm not gay." *I'm an inexperienced guy who is confused and scared and kind of intrigued by Deacon.*

Riker clicked his fingers and pointed at me. "Bi? Pan? Any of the others? We won't judge. I like guys. Nox will—"

"Enough," Deacon snarled, and I was grateful for it, though surprised that his harsh tone hadn't scared me.

Then again, my head was too busy spinning from confusion.

I seriously wanted to know what these three were playing at. Why did they come for me at college?

"I can see we've upset you. We'll talk it out at the coffee shop," Deacon said.

I glanced from Deacon, to Riker, then Nox, and back to Deacon. I honestly didn't know what to think, but I was 80 percent sure, no, 70 percent sure they didn't want to kidnap or hurt me.

Really, there was only one way to find out what they wanted.

Besides, it wasn't like I could say no either. Riker looked fast and the other two deadly. Plus, I was curious about what they wanted. Especially why Riker was interested in my sexuality in the first place.

Nodding, I gestured to walk on with a wave of my hand, and Deacon led the way, with Riker beside me again. Nox, the classmate, took up the rear.

Then it occurred to me that if Riker asked if I was gay, did that mean one of them was into me?

I stumbled a little but managed to stay on my feet. Riker chuckled beside me.

Holy fuck, what was I supposed to do with that thought? Now I looked guilty with Nox saying I drew Deacon's eyes. Wait, was it Deacon who was attracted to me?

Suddenly, my palms sweated as my pulse raced and gut twisted, but in a fluttery way that told me I wasn't too opposed to the idea of it being Deacon.

What the fuck am I going to do?

CHAPTER FIVE

RIO

*D*eacon held the door open and then pushed Riker aside to nod at me to enter first. More flutters started. The man was confusing me. Was he even gay? Well, I supposed he was if he really was interested in me.

I could be reading into it, though.

Maybe that was Riker's ability, to confuse their targets while they gained some trust before killing them.

Shit. Was I going to die?

I jolted when a hand landed on my lower spine.

I looked up at Deacon. "Relax. You have my word no harm will come to you."

Melty. That was the only word I could find that described the feeling in my body. "Okay," I whispered.

Did I sound needy, then?

Oh my fucking God. Maybe it would be best if they killed me.

Clearing my throat, I strode over to an available booth and slid onto the seat. It wasn't until Deacon took the spot next to me and I saw the other two take the spots opposite us, did I realize I'd just cornered myself around them.

Swallowing slowly, I reminded myself that Deacon gave me his word. When I glanced to him, he smiled gently and nodded.

My heart stumbled over its own beat and my cock twitched behind my jeans.

Had my libido finally kicked in to drum its own rhythm for the man next to me?

Why?

Great, now I was just dribbling shit in my own head. I'd been horny before over porn or if a woman brushed against me too close and gave me those sex eyes.

My urges weren't just for Deacon.

They weren't.

His arm went along the top of the booth behind me, and I nearly shot my damn load from his scent wafting my way.

Jesus, how could one man smell so good?

Wait... was he sniffing me also?

A low grumble left his lips and I spun wide-eyed to him.

"What's that about?" I demanded, pressing my back into the wall.

Riker snickered, but when Deacon shot him a glower, he looked to the ceiling.

Nox rolled his eyes. "I'm getting a drink."

"Oh, I'll have a hot chocolate and a blueberry muffin," Riker said with a clap.

Nox sighed and then stared at Deacon.

But when I glanced to him, he was already looking at me. "Would you like something to eat and drink?"

"Ah, yes?"

His lips tipped up in the corner. "What would you like?"

It was getting hot in here. I was sure they just turned up the heater. "Water, please."

Deacon turned to Nox. "Grab a bottle of water, a coffee, a cake, cookies, and a sandwich."

He must have been hungry.

Nox grunted and left the table.

When I heard Riker shift on his seat, I faced him to discover he stared back with his elbows on the table, arms up, and head rested on his hands. "So," he drew out, "do you like your daddy?"

"Excuse me?"

A growl sounded beside me, but when I eyed Deacon, he was watching Nox.

Had I imagined that sound?

I wouldn't be surprised. Stress still pumped throughout me and had my knee bouncing.

Back to Riker, I asked again, "Do you mean my father?"

"Yeah, your daddy."

Palming my face, I swiped my hand over it. "Please don't call him that."

"Okay." He grinned. "But do you like him?"

"Is this why you're here? You're wanting me to snitch on my father? I can't. If he found out, he'd kill me and my mother—"

Wood groaned and I looked down at the end of the booth where Deacon had a tight hold of the edge.

"Uh-oh," Riker muttered.

My hand shook as I reached out to place it on Deacon's other arm resting back on the table. His gaze flashed to me. "Are you okay?" I asked.

He made a different noise in the back of his throat, almost like a chuffing. My gaze dropped when his warm palm lay over my hand. A shiver raked over me and I licked my lips. Why did I feel warmer?

My cock throbbed.

Oh shit, that's just embarrassing.

Deacon ducked his head, and his nose brushed over my neck.

I panicked.

I shoved him away in fear but then pulled him back in toward me because he'd gotten too far away.

My breath panted out of me as I stared at his chest, trying to work out why I was acting like a lunatic.

"Rio," Deacon called lowly.

I lifted my gaze to see his pupils were blown wide.

"W-What's going on?" I squeezed his arms from where I still held them when I'd tugged him around.

Tugged.

Now I pictured my palm wrapped around his hard cock as I *tugged* him up and down slowly. I bit my bottom lip to stop the moan, but a sound still escaped.

Deacon inhaled deeply before more chuffing fell from

between his lips. At least that was what it sounded like to me. Almost as if he was a content animal, but that was crazy.

What was wrong with me?

A tray dropped to the table.

Jumping, I let go of Deacon, and faced Riker with my hands under the table, holding my thighs while I tried to catch my breath.

Why was I searching for oxygen in the first place? It wasn't like I just ran a marathon.

Riker laughed around a bite of his muffin. He nodded down in front of me, and I looked there. My eyes bulged.

In front of me, I had a coffee, water, sandwich, cookies, and cake.

Deacon's hand slipped into view and picked up a sandwich that looked like it contained meat and salad.

It rose and rose, stopping just in front of my mouth.

I glanced to Deacon out the corner of my eyes.

"You need to eat," he told me and, somehow, his words had me opening my mouth and taking a bite. He pulled his hand away and—for a reason I couldn't explain, because I didn't even know why I did it myself—I gave him a smile and two thumbs up.

"Aww, I want one as cute as him," Riker said.

What did that mean?

What was going on?

Deacon grumbled something and Nox snorted.

Deacon went to feed me again, which I was finding a little erotic.

Dear God, I needed fucking help.

I placed my hand on his wrist, halting him. "Can we, ah, please talk about why you guys are here?"

Deacon nodded and put the sandwich back on the plate. "If you still eat while we talk."

I flicked my gaze around to them all. "Sure."

This was really weird.

I didn't know what to think of them.

Deacon confused me the most.

My body had never reacted so quickly around someone before. Yes, I'd felt attraction, but not in a way where my dick was ready to act if Deacon wanted to get frisky.

Frisky?

Seriously?

And since it had been Deacon wanting me to eat, I picked up the sandwich and took another bite before waving it around.

Deacon grinned. "We need to know your thoughts about your father. We offered him a large amount of money to stop selling his supplies in our area and he disagreed. We've asked for more time to think of a better offer, but really it was so I could see if you have a fond connection to him."

"Shit's about to hit the fan," Riker sang.

I choked on the food in my mouth and Deacon had the glass of water waiting in front of my lips in seconds. A shudder went through me as he touched under my chin to help me tip my head back to drink.

What was that about? His attentiveness and my reaction to it.

Grabbing the glass out of his hand, I took another sip

and cleared my throat while watching him. Even his worried gaze puzzled me.

He was the biggest out of the three of them. Broader and slightly taller than Nox. Good-looking.... Okay, he was very good-looking. I could admit it. But maybe whatever was going on inside of me was like what I felt for my high school teacher. A crush of attractiveness.

Yeah, and then why am I thinking of humping his leg to prove he's with me, so those bitches stop looking at him?

There was a group of women not far from us staring, giggling, and waiting for his attention.

I flicked out a hand at them and when I got their attention, I shook my head and glared.

They scowled back but took their surveillance elsewhere.

Fingers pinched my chin. Deacon turned my head his way.

I wanted to come in my pants.

"Don't worry about them," he told me, smiling softly.

His finger was so close to my mouth and, fuck me, but I wanted to suck on that digit. My cock throbbed again.

A throat cleared.

Deacon flashed Nox a glare.

But at least it brought me out of my Deacon daze.

I needed to get away from this man and fast, before I took off all my clothes and told him to take me.

"Right, yes." I nodded to myself and shifted closer to the wall again. "Ah, back to what you were saying. I gather that, by Riker saying, 'shit's about to hit the fan,' it means you're thinking of going against my father by not paying anything and expecting him to comply to your wishes?"

Deacon nodded. "Yes."

"Are you fucking crazy?" I yelled.

When someone shushed me, I got to my knee and peered around the café for them with a narrowed gaze.

Deacon chuckled and dragged me down.

Eyes widening, I asked quietly this time, "Seriously, are you crazy?" Leaning in, I added, "You know who he is, right? Do you know the people on his payroll or how many people are under his thumb from all over the world? Your lives will be snuffed out within a week. No one goes against Santiago. *No one.* Because the ones who have tried are probably already dead."

Nox scoffed. "We'll handle it."

Clutching my gut, I arched over a little. "I feel sick." I touched my forehead. "I'm coming down with something. I'm delusional right now. That's why I can't stop with you." I waved a hand at Deacon. "It explains so much. I'm not really sitting here listening to this crazy idea." Laughing humorlessly, I shook my head. "They think they can go against him."

"He's losing the plot, like me," Riker chimed in with a cackle.

"Shut up," Deacon snarled.

My cheeks were squished between two large hands and my head was drawn up, my face right in front of Deacon's. I had to grab hold of his wrists in a tight grip because of the overload of lust pouring from me being this close. I shivered and panted out my breaths while trying to lick my dry lips, so they were ready for him.

I mean, the moment wasn't a good one to be kissing, but I was still on board.

"Rio, you don't know us, but I want to change that, and in doing so, you'll eventually trust us and believe that we'll have the situation at hand. No one here will die."

"Okay," I mumbled through squished mouth.

He searched my face before he nodded and relaxed his hold. "Do you fear your father?"

"Yes."

"Do you fear he will use your mother against you?"

"Yes. He has and will again."

Deacon's gaze hardened. "I won't let it happen, Rio."

"You can't—"

His hand slid over my cheek, so he could press his thumb against my lips. "Give me a chance. *Us* a chance to prove our strength to you, and with that chance, you will come under our protection. Not only for you, but your mother as well. Your father will no longer rule over you."

He was offering me what I wanted all my life. A world without Santiago's control over me.

CHAPTER SIX

DEACON

My mate's hands tightened around my wrists as his eyes glistened. My bear whimpered inside me, wanting to comfort our Rio.

Soon, I promised.

"You can't know the lengths he'll go to have control," he told me in a hushed tone.

"I do know."

"We need to move," Nox announced.

I dropped my hold and turned to the room, crowding Rio at my back. "Where?"

"Just came through the door. Two," Nox said.

"Riker" was all I said, and Nox moved out of the way to allow room for Riker to jump up with a laugh. I watched him skip over to the men and gain their attention.

Nox moved in front of me as I slid out of the booth to stand in front of Rio.

"What's going on?" he asked, the touch of fear scented on him.

I faced him. My larger and taller body covered his lean, but firm form wholly from where Santiago's men stood. "Men your father sent to follow you just walked in. We're getting you out of here without them noticing so we can talk more." I held out my hand. "Will you come with us?"

He glanced from my hand up to my face and nodded. My heart swelled. I fucking loved how his choice was instant.

Rio took my hand, and I helped him up from the booth as Nox moved to cover my mate while I turned to tuck him under my arm. Together, we got Rio out of the café without Santiago's men looking our way. It was also thanks to Riker for keeping their attention on him.

We rushed over the grounds to the parking lot where Nox unlocked our van and slid the back door open. I climbed in first in case Rio thought this looked like a kidnapping with the vehicle we had. He followed a little slower. Nox slammed the door shut before he got into the driver seat and started the car.

I tugged Rio onto the bench seat with my arm around his shoulders. It wasn't only his scent setting me off into protective mode, but how his body almost vibrated at my side.

"What's going on, what's going on, what's going on?" Rio chanted as he arched over to bury his face into his hands.

Rubbing at his back, my bear and I purred gently to relax him.

He swung around to me, nearly falling off the seat, and would have done if I hadn't grabbed for him.

"What's *that*?" He touched my chest and I stopped. "No, why do you make that sound? It's... I've never... no one does that."

In the front of the van, Nox snorted, and I wanted to hit him in the back of the head.

"I'll explain more at our place."

He shifted to face forward again, muttering, "I'm too trusting. They're going to kill me, and I willingly got into the van. My cock led me into danger. It's that big oaf's fault. He's weirding me out but making me mellow at the same time, which is freaking me out more."

Nox chuckled.

This time I did reach forward and hit him in the back of the head.

"Fuck," he yelled, shooting me the middle finger over his shoulder. It didn't matter that my hit may have hurt; no one laughed at my mate's expense. Especially when he didn't understand what was going on. It also seemed that the fated mate bond was helping his already present attraction toward me. He had drawn my eyes, after all. Though, I did wonder if the strong and fast buildup of desire had anything to do with him being a human. When shifters felt the bond, there wasn't much wooing in the process. We knew how rare the fated bond was and usually claimed one another instantly.

Rio looked back and forth from Nox and me, until he paused on me. "You couldn't hear what I was mumbling, right?" He was probably thinking it was humanly impossible to hear what he said since it *had* been low, yet we weren't fully human.

"I—"

The passenger door in the front opened and Riker bounced into it, hitting the dash. "Let's go, you hos." Riker sniffed and looked back at us. "What happened? Why does he smell uneasy, scared, and a little horny? I don't mind the horny smell—yes, I do. I fucking hate that smell. Please stop growling at me, Deacon." He whined. "I won't touch him."

Nox sighed, put the car into Drive, and moved out of the parking lot while I caught Rio as his brain overloaded and he passed out.

"You motherfuckers freaked him out," I snarled. My bear pushed at me, wanting out so he could scrape his claws through their underbellies.

"Sure, it was all us," Nox said, and I knew without looking he'd be rolling his eyes. "We weren't the ones who were all over him in the café. You two stank the place out."

I warred with myself over being pissed at him for saying that and smug for knowing I wasn't the only one who'd scented Rio's arousal for me.

"Shut up," I muttered half heartily as I gazed down at Rio. I had my arm tucked around his securely while his head rested against my shoulder. His head was tipped back a bit, nose pointed toward my neck.

My poor mate had been dealing with so much already and we just threw the shit about dealing with his father, commenting on his mumbling, and Riker's rambling on him as well.

"He was worried about us. That his father would take us down," Riker pointed out as he half turned in his seat to look at him. "I like him for you, brother."

My chest puffed up. "Thank you. I do too."

"Then you'll have to make him worry less, because it's annoying when he does," Nox said.

Riker blew out a raspberry. "You find everything annoying. You're boring, Noxxy."

"And you're a pain in the ass, Riker."

Riker grinned, clasping his hands under his chin. "You really think so? Thank you."

"Fuck off," Nox clipped.

"Enough," I ordered. "Be quiet until we get home so Rio can rest." I smoothed a thumb over his pinched brows. Thankfully my brothers listened. Then again, they'd do anything for him because he meant everything to me.

I WAS BEING CREEPY. I shouldn't be sitting here watching Rio while he slept in my bed. Yet, I couldn't stop myself. If I left the room, my bear was harder to deal with. I agreed with him, though: we didn't want Rio to wake alone in a strange room without a familiar face.

He'd have to like seeing my face first thing. He was my mate, but maybe hovering just above him as I watched him breathe was too much.

Nodding, I went to the armchair in the corner and dragged it over to beside the bed.

Leaning back, I picked up my phone from the bedside table for something to do.

But my gaze strayed back to Rio. My mate. My stunning mate.

My cock jerked under my jeans.

My bear chuffed.

He was excited for the claiming process, but I reminded him, once again, that we had to take it slow. Rio wouldn't be ready to jump between the sheets and to take my bite while I fucked him.

Would he let me fuck him?

I hoped so because I could already imagine sliding into his ass that I'd make slick from tonguing it. Fuck, I had to stop thinking about it. Reaching down, I strangled my hardness in my palm.

My animal was also keen to show himself to Rio. He wanted to rub his scent all over our mate. To sleep beside him, to have Rio pet him, and tell him how amazing he was.

Vain bear.

But I couldn't blame him. I wanted those things from Rio too. Except I could go without him telling me I was amazing. I wasn't that conceited. I also had murdering issues that I needed to see if Rio would accept.

Being a killer was a side of me I worried my mate wouldn't handle. Especially since I planned to end his father's life after all the suffering and neglect he'd put on his son. Anyone could see the damage, even without witnessing it themselves.

My phone chimed. I cursed and quickly silenced it. Rio stirred but didn't wake.

Looking to my phone and saw Ruth's name flash up. Sighing, I opened her text.

> You haven't reported in.

> > We haven't finalized things.

> Santiago's getting a product delivery at the end of the week. It'll get to the streets by the weekend, Deacon.

> > It won't.

> What's the delay?

Lifting my head, I smiled at Rio. Only for it to fade at the thought of Rio, for some reason, wanting to protect his father. Another text popped up. Ruth was getting impatient.

> ???

> > A complication. He didn't accept our offer.

> You know what must be done then.

To end him and his corporation. Another one could rise, but hopefully they'd be wise to listen to our demands.

> > I'll get it done.

> You're hiding something.

How the fuck did she know?

I'm not.

I'm calling Riker.

Fuck me, he'd cave and tell her. I stood and went to go to the door, but Rio made a noise, a soft mew. Just like a kitten.

It was adorable.

Christ. Ruth would have to wait.

His eyes fluttered and he stretched, then stilled as, no doubt, everything that had happened swept through his mind.

He peeked out one eye, saw me, and closed it.

Smiling, I sat on the edge of the chair and said, "I know it's a lot to handle. I know there are other thoughts running through your mind. Other possibilities that seem even strange for you. If you have questions, besides the obvious about your father, I'll answer them. I won't hide anything from you, Rio, and I'll also never hurt you. I'd rather take my own life before that."

His ocean blues landed on me as he pulled himself up to a sitting position and leaned against the headboard.

He grabbed at the T-shirt he wore that rested against his chest. "I feel it in here that you're telling me the truth. How is that possible?"

"Is that what you want to know first?"

He opened his mouth, closed it, and stared while he thought.

"First, I'd like to know are you seriously planning to take down my father and his illegal businesses?"

"Yes. Do you have any type of soft affection for him?"

"Fuck no." He blushed. "I mean no. I don't."

Relief flooded my body and my shoulders sagged. "Good."

"Why is it good?"

It was time to be honest. Even when it shot fear into my veins. Maybe it was too soon, and I should take my time with him, but I needed my mate to know everything to be able to accept me in his life.

Eventually.

After I wooed him a little longer.

"My brothers and I—"

"Brothers?"

I nodded. "In every way but blood."

"That makes sense since you look nothing alike."

Smiling, I shrugged and went on. "It does. Anyway, we work for a part of the government. A special branch that deals with... unsavory types like your father."

He leaned forward, gaze searching mine, wide and unsure. "Are you saying you and your brothers are planning to kill my father?"

I kept his gaze. "Yes, Rio."

He leaned back and laughed, slapping the bed. "Yeah, okay. And I'm Captain America." He shook his head, still chuckling. "Three guys against thousands. Sure, okay. You said this at the café, and I got scared, but you're just messing with me. Joking around."

I stared.

He blinked, sobering. "You are joking, right?"

"I'm not, Rio." *My mate.* "Are you going to be able to live with the knowledge of us ending you father?"

He looked down at his hands, fisting the sheet covering his lower half. "He's a bad person, Deacon."

My name from his mouth had me crowing on the inside. I wanted to hear it fall from his mouth in other situations too. Like when I slid—

Clearing my throat, I stopped those thoughts and answered, "Yes, he is."

"I've never wanted anyone dead. All I wanted was for him to leave Mamá and me alone." He looked up, eyes glistened. "But he won't, will he?"

"No. He's a selfish, corrupt, cruel man, Rio."

His jaw clenched. "If his life ends because of the things he's done, then so be it. This is your job. To make things better in the world. To stop the corruption."

"It is." I waited a beat before reluctantly adding, "It makes me a killer, Rio."

He nodded and swallowed. "I understand that, Deacon. It's not a job I would want, but if it's one you can do, who am I to judge?" His top teeth grazed over his bottom lip. "But I worry because I still don't see how the three of you can go against Santiago and his men."

Drawing in a deep breath, I ran a hand over my face. "I can explain that too. You see—" I paused and cocked my head to the side when I heard Riker running through the house.

I stood, turning toward the door and moving in front of Rio.

"What? What is it? Can you hear something?"

The door burst open, and Riker tumbled through. He bounced back up to his feet. "I couldn't help it. She knows. She was already on her way and now she knows!"

"Fuck," I clipped, glancing over my shoulder when two hands gripped the back of my tee. Rio knelt on the bed behind me.

"Who's coming?"

"Have you told him?" Riker asked, rocking back and forth on his feet. "Have you explained everything? You need to do it before she gets here. She won't take him away because you guys have a connection, but if he knows everything.... I don't know what I'm thinking. I'm just—I had two coffees while waiting for Rio to wake up and now I'm buzzing. Did you guys do it?" Riker stepped closer and I let out a growl.

"Deacon, what the hell are you doing and what is he talking about?" Rio demanded. He let go of me, climbed off the bed, and stood beside me with his hands on his waist.

"Oh, just this," Riker said and then started to strip.

Since he only wore shorts and a tank, he was naked quickly.

"Whoa," Rio cried, covering his eyes.

Wincing, I moved behind Rio and rested my hands on Rio's hips. In his ear, I said, "You might want to watch this."

His head tipped up to me. "Huh?"

I nodded back toward Riker where his fox now stood.

Rio slowly glanced back and yelled, "What the fuck?"

CHAPTER SEVEN

RIO

Riker was a fox shifter.

Nox was a tiger.

And Deacon was a fucking bear.

Shifters were real.

They weren't the only things popping out of fiction into reality.

Vampires and fae.

But I didn't care about those, though.

I stared at the floor while my head was on the verge of exploding, along with my heart because it hadn't stopped erratically beating.

No, my reaction wasn't about learning of vampires or fae.

It was the fact that I was in the presence of shifters.

Animals that could rip me apart in seconds.

But they haven't.

Which was true.

Did that mean they wouldn't?

I could believe that Deacon wouldn't hurt me. He had told me he'd rather end his own life over mine.

Which was....

Why had he said that?

Nope, think about that later.

When I wasn't wrapping my mind around Deacon, Riker, and Nox being able to shift into animals.

"Rio?" Deacon called softly from where he stood by the door with a dressed-again Riker, since I'd waved them away while I plonked on the bed and pondered everything.

Pondered.

What a weird word.

It wasn't time to think about that either.

"Rio, I know it's a shock, but we won't hurt you."

Deep down, I knew that.

But I just learned there were shifters in the fucking world, so I was allowed to freak the fuck out. Jesus. It hadn't even been five minutes.

I held up one finger.

Shifters were real.

R. E. A. L.

As in, I could pat them if I wanted to.

"Are you in control of your animals?" I asked to the carpet.

"Yes," Deacon replied.

Nodding, I pressed a hand to my chest.

"Even the bear?"

"He would never hurt you."

At his rough tone, I glanced up. "How can you be sure?"

He winced and glanced off for a beat before looking back at me with determination.

Riker rocked up and down on his feet. Onto his toes and back down. He clasped his hands behind his back and shot me a wink before I put my attention back on Deacon.

"Fuck!" Nox roared. "She's here. She's here."

Riker gasped. He seemed pleased, but also uncertain. "Do we hide him?" he asked Deacon.

The bear shifter took a step toward me and then back to the door again before moving over to me. "Yes. I think so. I don't know."

"Who is it?" I forgot their reaction from earlier since I'd learned about shifters. That kind of information tended to block out everything else.

Deacon stomped over to me, picked me up, and flung me over his shoulder. "You could say she's our mother," he said.

"The bathroom?" Riker suggested. He raced over there and opened the door, only to close it. "No, you do not want Rio to see the state you left it in."

"The closet," Deacon blurted and rushed around the bed to the walk-in closet.

"This is ridiculous," I shouted, gripping at the bottom of Deacon's tee, and trying to pull myself up as he spun this way and that, looking for a spot to hide me in the huge area. "First, you take me from college. Second, you say shit that scares me enough I pass out. Third, I wake up to you telling me you're going to kill my father. And last,

67

Riker shifts into a fox right in front of me and I learn you're a bear. It's too fucking much, Deacon," I snapped.

"I would have to agree," a woman said from the doorway she leaned against with her arms crossed. Dressed in jeans, boots, and a long-sleeved top, she seemed to be in her forties. There was no way she could be their mother.

I slapped Deacon's hip, since he was frozen and faced the other way from the entrance.

And even though I wanted to hide myself, I dug up some courage. Since this woman seemed important to Deacon, I felt the need to impress her or at least act like what was happening didn't faze me. Honestly, I didn't have a clue what I was doing. But I pushed up off Deacon's firm ass and waved. "Hi. I'm Rio. They said their mother was coming, but you can't be her. Are you Deacon's girlfriend?" My gut twisted at the thought of Deacon with someone.

The man who held me dry heaved and then picked me up off his shoulder like I weighed nothing, and placed me on my feet. He turned and held me in front of him with his hands on my shoulders.

"Ruth."

"What the fuck have you done, Deacon Blackwood?"

Oh, that sounded like a mother tone.

"Hi, Mom," Riker said, popping up beside her from somewhere and curling his arms around her waist.

Her expression softened as she hugged him to her. "Hello, sweetheart. Be a good fox and go make us a coffee." She cupped his cheeks, kissing his forehead. "And tell Nox to stop hiding. I want him in the kitchen in five."

"I will." Riker grinned and skipped off.

Ruth turned back to us, a glower back in place. "Deacon?"

"Rio is the son of Santiago. We're helping him and his mother before we take care of Santiago."

She crossed her arms over her chest and dropped her gaze to me. "No offense, darling." She looked back to Deacon. "Why?"

Yeah, why? I parroted inside my head.

"Because" was all Deacon said.

"Rio, be a dear and move into the bedroom."

I wanted to. I really did. But as soon as I took a step, Deacon pulled my back into his chest and wrapped his arms around my shoulders.

Warmth shot into my body. I knew my face heated, but my dick also took that very inappropriate moment to take notice of how much of Deacon actually touched me. His body was lined perfectly with mine.

Oh God, was that hardness at my ass?

Sweat formed at my brows. I needed to get away from him. His arms relaxed a little and then his hands landed on my shoulders again, but ran down my arms, leaving a trail of goose bumps.

My cock throbbed. I bit my bottom lip and dipped my head.

Ruth needed to leave before I came in my pants.

No. It was better if I ran. While his hold was loose, I bolted for the doorway, out of it, and stood in the middle of the bedroom and panted.

Glancing around the room, I looked for something, anything to focus on.

Smack.

I spun back toward the walk-in closet in time to see Ruth hit Deacon. Big, strong, intense bear shifter Deacon, in the back of the head.

"Tell me," she demanded.

"He's my fated mate."

What?

What did that mean?

Ruth's head shot back to stare at Deacon. "Are you sure?"

Deacon's grin was the biggest I'd seen on him yet, and his gaze shone down on her. "My bear and I are completely sure."

"Wait," I started, and when Ruth faced me, I pointed at Deacon. "What does *that* mean? Fated mate?"

She startled and glanced to Deacon. "He doesn't know?"

He squirmed under her gaze. "Everything you heard from Rio earlier is all that's happened."

"In one day?" she screeched.

Deacon ducked his head. "Yes." Then he raised it and added, "But to be fair, I only scented him last night on the job. I didn't want to scare him—"

"Scare him?" she yelled and punched him in the arm. "You idiot. You've turned up at his college after he saw you and your brothers sitting down with his father, who I'm sure he knows isn't a good man." She glanced back to me, and I nodded. She faced Deacon again. "And then you bring him here and Riker shifts in front of him. Of course, he's going to be scared." She kicked him in the shin. I would have been concerned about the violence, but Deacon didn't react, so I was sure none of it hurt him.

Ruth spun and walked my way. I let out a meep when she cupped my cheeks like she had Riker. "You sweet boy. I'm so sorry about what you've been through with these buffoons, but I can tell you deep down, deep, *deep* down, they're sweet and caring. They just don't think sometimes. You're in safe hands now. You have nothing to fear from us because you, my boy, are a treasure and will be spoilt like you should be."

Huh?

She smiled gently. "I'll leave Deacon to explain the mate part and see you downstairs later." She stared at me some more and her eyes started to tear up. "A true treasure." With a sniff, she turned back to Deacon, who had come out of the walk-in closet, and hugged him tightly before leaving the room.

When the door clicked closed, I turned to Deacon. "Is she really your mother?"

Deacon sighed and waved a hand toward the bed. "This could take a while. Would you sit with me?"

My stomach grumbled in that moment, and Deacon's eyes widened. I glanced out the window to see it was nearing dusk. I must have "napped" a lot longer than I thought. No wonder I was hungry.

"Whoa," I cried when I was scooped up bridal style, which had me blushing, and carried to the bed where Deacon planted me in the same spot I had been.

"Wait here. I'll get some food. I should have known you would be hungry. You hardly got to eat at the café." He smoothed a hand over my head and made his way over to the door. "I won't be long," he said before leaving. I then heard shouted, "He's hungry. My mate needs food."

A laugh escaped me, but it quickly dissipated.

I drew in a shuddering breath and ran a hand over my face.

My stomach fluttered because I'd already guessed what a fated mate meant to a shifter. I had a rough idea about mates from fiction I'd read. Deacon had been attentive to me and my needs since that morning. He'd told me I had nothing to fear from him or his brothers. He wanted to take care of anything that concerned me, and I had a feeling that wasn't just because the government had sent him after Santiago.

My pulse raced, and I pushed down on my stomach since it wouldn't quit with the flutters.

This was crazy.

Unbelievable.

But it was happening.

I was living it.

To Deacon, I was his fated mate, and that meant he and his bear saw me as his.

His lover, friend, and spouse.

"Holy fucking shit," I whispered while moving my hand up to my chest.

Smiling, I shook my head. I wouldn't admit to the giddiness rolling through me at the thought of Deacon seeing me as his. I couldn't as the ever-present doubt that had kept me safe, stopped the happy endorphins in their place.

What happened if he was wrong?

What happened if in the end he didn't like me?

What did I think of him?

A conjured image of Deacon Blackwood had my body

reacting in ways that made it clear there wasn't a chance I could deny I didn't like the man. Even in such a short amount of time, I knew I wanted him. There was a deep craving to see where a relationship between us could go. The thought of not trying scared me more than if my father found out I was here with the people who were going to take him down.

CHAPTER EIGHT

DEACON

"Wwhat about these things as well?" Riker came running from the pantry with an armful of different items. I wasn't sure why he held a bag of plain flour, though.

"I don't think so," I said, rubbing at the back of my neck while I hovered over Ruth as she cooked a stir-fry.

Would Rio like it? What did he prefer to eat? Was he allergic to anything? "What happens if he's allergic to what you're making?"

"I'll go ask him," Riker shouted and ran out of the room. I heard his heavy footsteps and then the door to my bedroom was flung open. Rio screamed. Riker yelled, "Are you allergic?"

"Allergic?"

"To food?"

"No, I don't have any allergies."

Riker thundered down the stairs again.

"Deacon," Ruth called.

"Hmm?" Was she adding too much salt?

"Relax. He'll eat it because he's hungry. You have time to find out what he prefers another day and provide it for him. For now, just get his belly full. Yes?"

"Yes. But is that too much salt?"

She sighed. "Do you want to take over?"

"Yeah." I grabbed the spatula out of her hand, and she moved out of the way with a laugh.

As I stirred the food, Ruth patted my arm. "You'll be a good mate for him."

I glanced out the corner of my eyes. "You think so?"

"Completely."

Good. "But will he accept me as I am?" *Someone who can kill without remorse.*

She leaned into the counter beside me. "He already knows what your plans are for his father, right?" I nodded. "The exact plan? That you and your brothers will kill Santiago and anyone else who stands in your way to clean up this area?"

"He does."

"The guy is already half in love with him. Isn't that what being a fated mate means? The choice is gone from you," Nox said from a corner.

"Good of you to come out, son."

He grunted.

"You're wrong, Nox," Ruth said. "Being a fated mate doesn't mean your choice has been taken away. It's a gift yes, but one you can decide to take on. If the attraction isn't there to begin with or if one partner isn't liked by the other, the link won't take. Fate wouldn't force another on you. Yet, it seems Deacon's human found something in Deacon that intrigued him enough for a slight connection to form. Though, I've never witnessed it, but there is a rumor that humans tend to have a higher reaction to their fated *if* they're first attracted to their one and are treated as the treasures they are. If their fated doesn't treat them with the utmost care, no matter being human or not, the link won't bloom." Ruth picked up the salt and tried to put more in, but I moved the pan out of the way, which had her laughing. "That being said. I have done my own research into fated mates. Fate doesn't fuck around, Nox. They know what they're doing, and from what I've learned, there hasn't been a fated couple who hasn't worked out. Even if they've come from different worlds."

Nox said nothing, but I heard him move so I presumed he tipped his chin up at Ruth.

"I hope I get a fated mate," Riker announced as he came back into the kitchen. "Also, I'm sure you heard, he's not allergic to anything. But he did say he doesn't like bears. He prefers foxes. Go figure."

Turning, I threw the knife I'd picked up from the counter. Riker, unfortunately, jumped out of the way just as it embedded into the wall where he'd been standing.

"Deacon," Ruth scolded. "And Riker, don't tease a shifter when it comes to their fated. As you can see, things will get serious very quickly."

Riker chuckled. "I know. Isn't it fun!" He skipped out of the way with a laugh when I threw another knife at him.

With a sigh, I grabbed a plate out and dished up food for my mate. I had to get out of here before I did kill someone. I didn't like knowing my mate was hungry upstairs. He needed, I provided, but this was taking too long. When I made sure Rio had the best-looking pieces of meat in his portion, I plated some for myself.

"I'm going," I told them.

"Wait," Ruth called. She grabbed two forks and slid them under the food. Then took two bottles of water out and tucked them under one arm before patting me there. "Good luck." She smiled.

My pulse picked up. "Thanks."

"He didn't leave me any," Riker complained.

Ruth snorted. "You guys never change. Come on, sweetheart. I'll make you something."

I heard his clap as I reached the stairs, and then my focus went to the man in my bedroom. Rio wanted to know what fated mates were, and I would tell him, but I couldn't stop the bitterness of fear thickening my throat if he decided he didn't want anything to do with me. And from what Ruth said, even though a small link had formed, it seemed Rio had the chance to back out of this deal of a life with me.

Already I was all in. He'd stolen my whole being when I first scented him, and no other would do. But I wouldn't force myself on someone. My bear would just have to accept our mate's choice in the end. No matter what it would be.

If Rio didn't want us, there was a chance I'd have to be locked up for a bit, but I would exile myself for him.

My heart hammered behind my ribs as my bear paced inside me.

Riker had left the door open so when I entered, my gaze went straight to Rio sitting on my bed where I'd left him. His small smile aimed my way, tightened my chest.

Christ, he was stunning.

"Sorry to keep you waiting," I told him, handing over the plate.

His eyes flared. "You didn't.... This is, ah, a lot."

"If you don't eat it all, I'll finish it. But eat what you can." I put my plate on the bedside table while I handed a bottle of water over to him and placed mine on the floor. I picked my dinner back up and waited for Rio to taste his first. "If there's too much salt, that's Ruth's doing. I took over when I thought she was overdoing it."

"Okay. Thank you." He nodded, picking up his forkful and guiding it to his mouth. Red coated his cheeks, and I realized it was probably because I stared intently at him while he chewed. "Good," he said with a nod.

I started in on mine and we ate in silence.

What was he thinking?

Did he like my room?

Would he want to move in here?

I knew he had a mother to consider, but I was a little pissed at her for leaving her son to deal with Santiago while she lost herself to other substances. It was selfish. Still, if Rio wanted her around, in this house, I would accept her into our home. She'd be far enough away that maybe she'd get lost walking around.

"Do you think we could check on my mamá later?"

She didn't deserve his loyalty.

"Yes." I placed my plate onto the floor, having finished.

"Thank you." He blew out a breath and held out his plate that had some left. I took it with a smile and ate what was left while he watched me with heat to his cheeks while I used the fork that had been in his mouth.

My bear and I didn't mind Rio staring. We wanted him thinking of our mouth and all the pleasure we could give him.

He took a gulp of water, and I watched it go down his throat. Of course, my mind turned to other things going down his throat. Would he drink my cum? Could he consider it? Would he like it? I'd scented arousal from him, but would that be enough to give him enough courage to kiss, hug, make love?

"So," he drew out. "Fated mates?"

Humming, I nodded and put his plate on top of mine. I quickly drank water and wiped over my mouth.

"Fated mates are.... You see...." How did I explain this?

What was the best way to tell him that if he were to choose me, I would make him never regret that decision? I would dote on him for the rest of our lives. He would never want because I would already have it. He would never be scared because I would fight his battles.

He would be mine, and I his.

I blinked down at the sheet when his fingers slid into view.

"Deacon?"

I pulled my gaze up to his warm blues. "Rio?"

"You're a shifter."

79

Was he still worried about my animal? "We would never hurt you in either form."

"I've gathered." He nibbled at the corner of his bottom lip. But then drew in a breath, and said, "I'll be honest. It'll take me some time to get used to, with you being a shifter. Actually, it isn't about *you* being a shifter, more the fact that there are shifters and other things in the world. But for now, I want to let you know I've read books before. Yes, they may have been fiction, but... I don't like to see the worry in your eyes when you try to find the right words to explain fated mates. So, to let you off the hook, and tell me if I get this right, does being fated mates mean that you're wanting me as... um, yours? Like, a lover, or maybe a husband?"

Thump.

Thump.

Thump.

He knew.

It didn't matter how he'd learned.

He hadn't run from the house screaming at the thought of being fated to me.

Rio's smile grew. "I just shocked you."

"You're still here," I stated in awe.

He flushed again. "I am."

I clenched my fists on my thighs to stop from reaching for him.

He was still here.

Could I possibly hope?

My bear chuffed. He thought I was stupid for doubting our mate. Of course, he would want us.

I stood, sat back down, and stood again. "It's a lifelong

connection between us." I turned, shoved the chair away where it hit the wall and knelt beside the bed. "Rio, fated mates are rare for our kind and other species. If you accept this between us, I will take care of you until our end of days." My skin tingled from how buzzed I felt having Rio consider the possibility of accepting me. "I understand you'll need time for the idea of having me in your life. Having me as your other half, and I'll give you all the time you need, but... you are thinking of this, yes?"

I had to hear it from his sweet mouth.

His hands ran over the sheet on his lap, straightening it out. "There are things you need to know too." A blush rose to his cheeks and spread down to his neck.

"You can tell me anything, Rio."

"My years haven't been easy. I knew that having Santiago as a father I had to be careful of who I brought into my life. I never trusted that Santiago would allow me to have a friend or partner without giving him a means to use them in some way. For this reason, I've kept my distance with everyone. I don't have friends, Deacon. I've never had a partner."

My heart shattered.

My bear keened.

Sorrow bled into my veins for my mate.

"You no longer have to be scared of him." This was a promise.

"It's hard to believe that, Deacon."

"Then wait until I can prove it to you. My bear and I are fierce. With my brothers, we are unstoppable. With their help, I will see to it that your father will never interfere with your life again. You'll be able to do as you wish, gain friends if you want. There'll be no more hiding in fear of consequences. I *will* make sure of it all, Rio." Slowly, I reached out and ran the back of my hand over his on the sheet he gripped.

"Deacon," Rio whispered, tone thick.

I lifted my gaze and saw moisture there. I raised my hand and glided a big digit across his cheek. "You'll always be protected, and I'm not saying this because I don't think you can take care of yourself. But you've been on your own trying to fight a battle against many, with no one at your back. You now have me and my brothers."

"Fuck you, you big shifter," he blurted before I was attacked.

He leaped at me, arms around my neck, and hugged me close, burying his forehead into my shoulder. I closed my arms around his waist and held tight.

He'd never had anyone.

Until now.

I would be everything he needs.

CHAPTER NINE

RIO

Jesus Christ.

How could one person fill me up so much while it felt like I was bursting with goddamn mushy emotions? Already I knew Deacon would make me crave more, and I'd gladly accept them because I'd never been so full before.

So complete.

No one had made me near combust from happiness and goodness in all my years.

Not even when I was younger and things hadn't been so bad.

Never content, until I was in this moment.

Could I really believe and trust this connection was at my fingertips, and all I had to do was reach out and take it?

"Why are you laughing?" Deacon asked as he rubbed his cheek into the top of my head.

"Because you're already in my grasp."

He paused. "Sorry?"

I shook my head into his shoulder. "Nothing."

"Okay," he whispered and went back to gently rubbing his cheek against me.

This man was an intimidating mountain of a man and yet here he was holding me with such softness that made me feel special.

Fuck me.

I *was* special to him.

Me.

Rio Santiago.

And there *I* was clinging to this mountain of a man. I'd never held onto someone before. Even Mamá didn't like to be touched or hugged by me.

Deacon Blackwood wanted me.

My gut fluttered. My dick throbbed.

Pulling back, I ran a hand over my hot face and glanced at him out the corner of my eye. "What happens if Fate fucked up and—"

"No. Never. Fate knows what it's doing, and I can have Ruth explain it better, but in a roundabout way, this link between us wouldn't be growing if there wasn't an attraction and some type of trust already."

Groaning, I pressed against my chest, even knowing it wouldn't stop my fast-beating heart. "Deacon...."

"What?" He reached out and took my hand from my chest, holding it between his larger ones.

"I've never been with anyone."

"Are you worried you won't like it? Are you worried you'd prefer a woman?"

An abrupt laugh escaped me. "No. Well... no. I don't know. I worry I won't be enough. What happens if I like to, ah... Christ, top?"

"Then you fuck me."

If I wasn't hot already, I was burning now at the image conjured.

"Really? It's that simple? Your animal won't mind?"

God, was I getting ahead of myself already talking about sex?

My cock was painfully hard now.

Deacon drew in a breath, his pupils dilated, and he grinned. "My bear and I will take your pleasure any way you want to give or take it."

Shaking my head, I scratched at my neck. "I can't believe I'm talking about this with you when we only met today."

A shiver raked over me when he cupped the side of my neck. "Don't be embarrassed, Rio. Our connection is growing. Share anything and everything you wish. And if anyone makes you feel awkward, I'll kill them."

The last part was said with such ferocity, I believed him.

"You can't kill everyone who might upset me."

His gaze darkened. "I can. I will."

The air in the room tightened.

I swallowed thickly at the realization that Deacon would actually harm anyone who messed with me. If he hadn't already been given the kill order by the government for my father, then I could see Deacon taking on Santiago and his army just to keep me safe.

Holy shit.

I'd never wanted to kiss someone like my life depended on it.

I dug up my courage, reached out to him while I pressed my lips against Deacon's.

When a low growl started in his chest, I threaded my fingers through his hair and tilted my head slightly, deepening the kiss. A gasp escaped me when he pushed me back on the bed with his mouth, his body, and hands. He took the opportunity to thrust his tongue between my lips. My cock fucking ached to be touched. I shamelessly and inexperiencedly ground up on him.

A noise, like a purr, formed in the back of his throat as we kept kissing.

I ran my hands over his broad shoulders, his back, until he pulled away to stare down at me.

"Fuck," he clipped. "Fuck."

"What?" I asked breathlessly.

"You kissed me."

Smiling, I nodded. "I did."

The color of his eyes deepened. "Our mate. We'll make you happy like you already do us."

Sliding my shaky hand to his cheek, I told him, "I believe you."

His mouth was back on mine, and we groaned into each other.

Deacon rolled and I was suddenly on top of him, staring down with a laugh. "What are you doing?"

His gaze flicked down to my groin. "You're hard."

Feeling brave, I rocked back on his large length. "So are you."

He sucked in a sharp breath before another growl rumbled out. "Let me taste, mate. Please. Just a taste? Let me give you pleasure."

What did he mean?

My heart stuttered.

"H-How?"

His hands gripped my ass, and he pulled me up his body where my jean-clad dick was in front of his face.

"Take it out," he ordered.

And even though my nerves were getting the better of me, causing my body to tremble, I undid the button and slowly slid the zipper down. Deacon watched like I was revealing his favorite meal. One he would eat over and over again.

"Pull your cock out." His tone was deeper, gruffer.

Reaching in, I gripped my cock, causing a moan to drop from my lips.

His hands tightened on my ass, nudging me forward. I pulled my leaking prick free and grabbed the headboard with one hand. I used the other hand to hold my tee out of the way, moaning when Deacon ate me down to the back of his throat. He sucked and tongued all around me while he grabbed my hips and helped me slowly withdraw from his wet lips. The help was needed as I was lost in the pure bliss of feeling him surrounding me.

It was much better than my own fist.

"Deacon," I whispered.

He hummed, which had me curling my toes into the bed. Deacon pushed and pulled at my hips, guiding me in and out of his mouth, and watching *my* dick in *his* mouth was something I wanted to see all the time.

Christ, I even had a thought of painting my cum over his body so it could soak into his skin and everyone would scent me on him.

I wasn't sure where that thought had come from, and I didn't care. I knew Deacon would let me. He'd want me to have anything. And I wanted to gift him the same, because receiving that kind of devotion was like a rush.

My head rolled back, I moaned, "Deacon."

When his fingers brushed over the crack of my ass, I lost it and cried out his name again as my cum shot down his throat. I probably should have warned him, but sensation had swept over me instantly.

Deacon picked me up and curled me over his body. I breathed heavily and patted at his chest.

"I liked that," I told him with a ragged voice.

His chuckle moved my head up and down. His arms tightening around me. "I'm glad, mate." He ran his fingers through my hair. If I were a kitten, I would have purred and slept. But there was something else I wanted to do instead.

A wave of shyness had me pressing my forehead into his chest. "I want to do it back to you," I admitted. My mouth watered at the idea of having Deacon's dick in my mouth. Returning the pleasure that he gave me.

Hell, I wanted us naked, to see his skin, to feel him. The need for it had me trembling.

His fingers stilled. "Don't feel you have to, Rio. You've never—"

Anger erupted, dimming the need. I lifted my head

and dug my chin into his nipple, glaring. "And you have? No, don't remind me of it."

He tapped my nose. "I like the jealousy, but it's misplaced because no one before you mattered. You're all I see, hear, and feel."

My sour mood swept away.

Damn, he was good.

Rolling my eyes, I muttered, "Okay." I glanced away and then back. "Will you sit up and feed me your—"

Oxygen left my lungs as I was moved off Deacon as he sat up, pulled his tee off, and undid his jeans. In the next second, I was picked up and placed between his spread legs on my knees.

"Yes," he growled.

A smile built before laughter burst out of me. I bent, holding my gut, until the humor fled when Deacon cupped the back of my head and dragged me forward where he claimed my mouth in a hot and wild kiss.

I pulled away, licking my lips and tasting myself on them. A salty, tangy flavor and one I could get used to if it always came from Deacon's mouth. Though, I couldn't wait to compare it to Deacon's own taste. So, even though I wanted to have his mouth again, I slid down the bed, so I lay on my stomach and rested up on my elbows. Seeing Deacon's chest rising and falling rapidly gave me a boost of confidence. With a shaky hand, I ran it up his thigh, over his hip, and down into his jeans. He lifted a little to push them down his hips while I released his long, thick cock. Before I let the nerves get the better of me, I licked over and around the tip.

Savoring his sweeter flavor than mine.

Deacon shuddered and a low rumble rolled out of him as he stared down at me with such hunger.

If I didn't know he had an animal inside of him, I'd be questioning it now.

Opening my mouth, I rested his knob on my tongue and closed my lips around him to suck.

"Christ," Deacon clipped darkly as his hands fisted the sheets.

I swiped my tongue around the outside and then up and down the front. His dick jerked in my hand.

"Rio," Deacon said through clenched teeth.

My gut danced; my dick throbbed. I sucked him down greedily and gagged. His fingers threaded through my hair, and he pulled me off him or I would have stayed and worked out how to open my throat, wanting him deep. I wanted to drink him down and feel him in the back of my throat.

"Fuck, Rio," Deacon bit out, searching my face.

"More." I licked my lips.

His growl was low, deep, but I got what I wanted when he released his hold on my hair and glided his fingers through it while I went down and swallowed him back in. Dipping up and down over him, I managed to open my throat more with each time I gagged and drooled over him. He groaned and swore, rubbing his hands over my hair, neck, shoulders.

"Mate, off," he warned, but it was unnecessary. I desired to taste him as he had me. I pulled back a little and felt his thighs under my hands tense before the first squirt of his cum drenched my mouth, followed by more and more that I drank down.

I licked around him, wanting more of his taste. Craving him. Desperate for him.

Hands threaded under my arms, and I was up, sitting on Deacon's lap while his arms wrapped around me, holding me close.

Smiling, I curled mine around his shoulders and kissed his neck.

Rapture had me squeezing him tighter.

He was mine.

All mine.

I wouldn't give him up.

I wouldn't be scared.

Deacon had made me feel more in a day than anyone ever had.

What we shared was different from regular people. We had a connection, a link that locked us together on a level that was more than a typical relationship.

Already I would do anything to keep what was growing between us.

CHAPTER TEN

DEACON

*T*aking Rio's hand as I opened the bedroom door, I glanced back and grinned. His lips were a little swollen, but I liked seeing them like that. I especially loved that blissed-out look when he had my dick in his mouth. As if he'd been needing it more than his next breath. Next time, I wanted to come over his face and rub it into his lips, his skin.

My bear chuffed at the idea, wanting that also, eager for our scent to soak into him more than it already was.

Rio glanced down at our hands and blushed.

Everything was new to him.

In one way, knowing I would be giving him all his firsts made that possessive, dominating side of me settle and caused a thrill to run up my spine. But in another way, anger weaved through my body. He'd been living half a life, a lonely existence because of Santiago, and I couldn't wait to peel my mate's father apart slowly for making Rio suffer.

For now, I pushed that anger aside. It could wait until I had that man in front of me.

I wanted to focus on my mate.

The voices of my family trailed off when we approached the dining area. I noted that as we entered, Riker was already turned toward us with a crooked smile. Ruth beamed at us, and Nox stared blankly but gave me a nod. They knew that with my scent on Rio, the talk had gone well.

My chest puffed up.

"I guess you're into guys after all," Riker said with a chuckle.

My bear bristled. Woodenly, I turned to see Rio's face on fire like I knew it would be.

Picking him up, I placed Rio to the side of the room.

"Deacon," Ruth said.

Riker clapped and jumped from the chair to the ground. "He looks like he enjoyed it."

"What's going on?" Rio asked.

But my bear drowned it out as he roared inside me.

I let him out.

The shift took only moments, and the room shook as my bear roared, swiping at Riker as he shifted down into his fox form and ran toward the exit. He was planning to escape outside, to get away from the punishment.

"Deacon," my mate yelled.

But no one embarrassed him.

No one.

With another roar, I rushed after the tittering fox.

"Rio, it's okay. Let them go," Ruth said.

My bear halted at the doorway, and we looked back at Rio.

Mate.

The fox would get his own, but we were more interested in our mate. Turning, we knocked into the table and a chair as we made our way up to Rio. We rubbed our nose into his stomach and brushed our head at his sides. Chuffing.

Our mate glided his hands through our fur.

We picked up the sound of the fox approaching. He wasn't as sneaky as he thought. We turned and swiped out at him with a growl. He danced back, but we clipped his leg and he tumbled.

With a huff, we sat down in front of our mate and watched the fox.

"Um," our mate said, patting our back.

"Riker, don't be a dick and change back," Nox said.

"And don't say anything to tease Deacon's mate or *I'll* take you out the back and deal with you," Ruth added.

Our mate leaned over our back, laughing slightly. "Wow, this is... you're such a beautiful sight. He's a bear," he said to the room, sounding amazed and happy.

"He is," Ruth replied. "It's good to see you're smiling, Rio. I'm presuming you want to try this bond with my son?"

I sent her a huff. We didn't like her questioning him in case he didn't want to talk about it.

She rolled her eyes. "Relax. Rio doesn't mind talking to me. Do you, dear?"

He cuddled into me, and we enjoyed knowing he wasn't scared. He liked us in both forms.

"I don't mind." He moved around and stood at my side. Reaching up, he placed his hand on my head. I snuffled into his neck, which had him grinning. "And yes, ma'am, I would like them as my mate."

Them.

Both of us.

His acceptance had us brimming with satisfaction, pride, and pleasure.

Riker made a noise before he shifted back into human. While our mate was distracted with the brother, we morphed also, so I could take him into my arms and hug him close.

Rio let out a sound somewhere between a laugh and sigh.

"Aww, aren't they cute?" Riker said.

Ignoring him, I brushed my nose along Rio's neck, drawing in his scent.

Mine.

"Riker, put clothes on before sitting down," Ruth demanded.

"Boo, being naked is freeing. You know, if I get a mate, I'm going to be naked all the time so he can—"

"Riker," I clipped with my bear present. I placed Rio on his feet and could feel him glancing from my brother to me, but I didn't look away from Riker until I got what I wanted.

Finally, he stared to the floor and bared his neck to me.

I grunted and Riker skipped off to get dressed while Nox stood and went to the window seat that held storage.

He grabbed me out some pants and a tee to throw at me. Riker had probably already used the clothes in the seat and forgot to replace them, like always.

Slipping them on, I held Rio's hand. "We're heading out to check on Rio's mom."

Ruth's brows rose. "Is that wise?"

"Santiago's watching," Nox added.

"I can't not check on her," Rio said.

"Would you let me go?" Ruth asked.

"I...." Rio glanced from Ruth to me and then shrugged. "I'm just used to doing it." His brows pinched. "I'm used to being the only one." His jaw clenched.

I cupped the back of his head and drew his front into mine, nodding at Ruth.

Rio pulled away from me and swore. He ran a hand over his face and turned to Ruth again. "Thank you. I'll come with you so she's not difficult—"

"No," I stated quickly and gruffly.

He looked to me. "No?"

Nox coughed to hide his chuckle, which he cut off quickly.

"Santiago will be watching your house," I told my mate.

"And? It won't be the first time. He likes to find new ways to keep me under his thumb."

"Deacon, I'll be there. Nothing will happen to your mate," Ruth said.

I ground my teeth together. Uncertainty had my fingers twitching. I wanted to grab him again and lock him away from everyone who could hurt him.

"Mamá won't trust a stranger. I need to be there."

I studied him and knew I wouldn't get anywhere if I tried to argue. There was a defiant gleam in his gaze. "You'll come back?"

"I... I don't know. I don't like leaving her alone."

His heart was too pure.

"I'll stay with her until this business with Santiago is done," Ruth said. "If she will allow it. Then your mate can come back to you, Deacon, if he wishes."

Rio blushed but nodded. I held down the chuff of contentment, knowing he wanted to be by my side as much as I did his.

Turning to Ruth, I asked, "Won't Grey want you home?"

Ruth smiled, and I wasn't sure I liked it. "Oh, I'm not leaving until I get to know my son's mate better. Besides, Grey will be here in the next few days, after he takes care of matters at his work."

She was staying.

"We have no room here," Nox lied.

Ruth shot him a glare. "Grey and I will be staying at the holiday house." Under her breath, she muttered, "Ungrateful little shits." And then she added louder, "You know I can still kick your ass, Nox."

Ruth's wolf in the past had been more dominant than our animals. Plus, she was a little crazed. But over time, she'd mellowed. She knew it. We knew it. But she got a little defensive of it.

"Yes, Ruth," Nox answered.

"Rio, let's go. And on the way, I can tell you things about these three."

I paled and gripped my mate's shoulders. "Don't believe anything she says."

Rio grinned and patted my stomach. My cock noticed how close his hand was to that area and thickened. "Don't worry."

He didn't understand. Nox, Riker, and I had been devils when we were younger. We always got into trouble.

"See, Nox, you must respect your mother more or you'll be in Deacon's shoes and shitting yourself from worry over what I'll say to your mate."

"I won't have a mate," he said, glancing out the window with a tight jaw.

"We'll see," Ruth said, walking from the room.

Rio went to his toes, kissed me quickly, flushed, and rushed after Ruth. I stared after him, fighting myself and my bear from following. At least Ruth's wolf would be stronger than any man I sent, and she would do everything she could to protect my treasure.

"When do we go after Santiago?" Nox asked.

"The sooner the better," I said, my animal riding my harder tone.

"Tomorrow?"

"Make the call. Tell him we have another offer."

"Got it." Nox nodded and left.

The new offer Santiago couldn't refuse.

Well, he wouldn't be able to because this one ended with his life.

Riker pranced into the room with a grin. "Yay to a bloodbath tomorrow."

"You're lucky Rio didn't mind your teasing, brother."

He looked at me coyly, digging his toe at the oak floorboards. "I know. But I'm sure he'll love me like you do."

Growling, I gave him a pointed look.

He rolled his eyes. "I don't mean *love* love me. Geesh, I wonder if I'll be this prickly when I get my fated mate."

If Riker got a fated mate, the world had better brace. He didn't have the ability to see reason when he was beyond pissed about something. Nox and I were the only ones who could get him to come back from a mindless blitz.

I worried what would happen if we weren't around when he lost himself.

Thankfully, that hadn't happened.

Yet.

Riker sidled up beside me. "Are we just going to stare at the doorway until your Rio gets home?"

Fuck. I hadn't even realized I had been.

"No," I bit out. I walked from the room back into the kitchen. Rio could be hungry when he got back. I'd make him something again. It would at least keep me busy instead of watching the door.

Dammit, I forgot to ask what his favorite food was.

CHAPTER ELEVEN

RIO

*M*y gut twisted. I'd made the wrong choice. I shouldn't have Ruth with me. I knew it as soon as I unlocked the front door and smelled the alcohol.

Wincing, I glanced back at Ruth. "Maybe you should wait here?"

The sympathy in her gaze stabbed at my chest. Being a shifter, she had a better nose than me; she wouldn't have missed the smell.

Shifter.

I still couldn't believe it. Then again, I could because I saw Deacon in his bear form.

He was the biggest bear I had ever seen, well, from what I could remember when I was younger and visited the zoo with school, but I couldn't think about Deacon

100

now. Not when I felt sick taking Ruth to witness what Mamá would say or do.

Ruth lay a hand on my shoulder. "I've raised three psycho shifters, dear. I can handle one drunk woman who is lost in life because of her ex."

"I don't know," I whispered.

"Rio" was called from down the hall. "Get in here." "Here" had sounded like "ear," so if the smell hadn't given away how intoxicated she was, her slurred words would have.

Slowly, I made my way down the hall and stepped into the open-plan living, dining, and kitchen. Mamá sat on the floor in front of the couch with pictures surrounding her.

Fuck me, it was one of those nights.

"You know he wouldn't have left me if I didn't have you. He never wanted a child. Always wanted to pick who would take over his world. You failed him being the quiet, soft child you were. So you failed me too. I'd still have him, if it wasn't for you. He'd still love me if my body wasn't marked because of you. He'd—"

"Enough," Ruth snapped.

Mamá jolted and blinked at the woman beside me. "Who the fuck are you?" she slurred before firing off rapid Spanish at me. About how I'd failed her again for not telling her we had a guest. But I was also stupid for bringing someone into her home.

She wobblily got to her feet and shuffled my way.

Ruth stepped in front of me and Mamá paused.

"Get out of my way." She waved her hand to the side. Another rant started in Spanish.

"Ruth, it's fine. She doesn't know what she's saying. She just needs sleep."

Ruth shook her head. "This is obviously not the first time she's spoken to you like this, Rio."

My mouth snapped closed when she looked over her shoulder at me.

"As I thought. A mother should never blame a child for their situation, no matter the circumstances." She looked back to the woman ranting as spittle flew out of her mouth, because we weren't paying her attention.

"Mamá, stop."

"Stop? You think you can tell me what to do like your father? You useless piece of trash. I should have—"

"Silence," Ruth clipped, and to my utter shock, she listened. "You do not speak to your son this way. If he was anything like Santiago, I would understand, but he's not. Even in the short amount of time I'd known him, I can see what a good soul your boy has. I will not tolerate what you're saying to him because of your own anger and self-loathing." Ruth turned to me. "I'm sorry, my dear, but I believe it's best you leave me here while she's like this. Deacon will not want you around hurtful words like that."

Shit.

Fuck.

Emotions clogged my nose. I sniffed, but worried it was useless to fight it.

No one had ever had my back.

No one understood what I was dealing with.

Until now.

Tears filled my eyes.

"Please, Rio, for my son's sake, leave your mother in my trust. If Deacon...." She shook her head. "Know I will handle her with care. She won't come to any harm by my hand or anyone else's."

I wiped at my face. "Ruth, I-I can't leave you to—"

She placed her hands on my shoulders. "Believe me when I say that this is the best scenario for everyone involved. Deacon would never harm your mother, either, but if he heard the lies she spewed about his mate, well, I doubt your mother would care about her son-in-law like I do mine." Her smile was gentle.

My heart clenched.

I didn't want to be a burden, though.

"Rio, my dear, sweet boy, you've dealt with this for too long already. You've accepted my son. You have a new family to go with the old, if she sees sense. Lean on us. Let us help."

My pulse raced as I stared at Ruth.

One day.

In one day my life was altered.

I wasn't alone.

I had people I could trust.

All I had to do was accept it.

"Okay," I whispered.

"Rio, what's this? What's going on? Who is this woman?"

Ruth smiled. "Thank you. I didn't sense anyone in this area when we entered. Go to the car and take it back to Deacon. Nowhere else, yes?"

"Yes, Ruth."

"Good."

"Rio, you're not leaving me with this stranger. Explain yourself."

I went to look to her, but Ruth tipped my chin away. "Go on now. I've got this."

Nodding, I took a step back, then another, and while Mamá started yelling, I turned and ran to the front door.

With each step, a weight slipped from my body to the floor, and my chest didn't feel so tight when I breathed.

WHEN I SAW Deacon already standing in the garage with the door open as I drove up their driveway, I knew Ruth had called ahead.

My body hummed at the sight of him.

He was mine.

I never thought I could think that about someone, but I was.

In a sense, I was free.

Freer than I'd ever been.

Shit, it almost had me floating over to a thin-lipped, worried Deacon after I got out of the car.

"Are you all right?" he asked, cupping my cheeks.

I placed my hands over his. "Yes. Your mom is great."

He leaned in and kissed my temple, causing me to shiver. "I'm glad she went with you, then."

As I was, because for once, I wasn't worried about Mamá. I didn't have that lead weight pressing down on me over worrying about rushing home to see what I had to clean up. She wasn't in my ear yelling at me.

Ruth chose to take care of her drunkenness for me.

Smiling, I nodded and pressed my face into his chest. How had I thought that this guy was going to kill or kidnap me?

Now, I was trying to melt into him. Into his warmth and comfort. I wanted to get lost in everything that was Deacon because he sent my emotions into a tailspin.

"Are you sure you're okay?" Deacon asked again.

Pulling back, I told him, "Yes. I've never felt at ease in my life, but I do here, with you."

His gaze softened. "I'm glad, mate."

"Rio," Riker whined from somewhere. "Deacon won't let us eat before you. Can you come in now, please?"

"Riker—" Deacon started, but I silenced him with a chaste kiss, because I could and because I wanted to. Gripping the back of my neck, he drew me in. But I knew we'd get carried away.

"We're coming in, Riker." I stepped away, took Deacon's hand, and led him into the house. Riker stood in the kitchen with Nox. They both stared down at the tray of chicken schnitzels and homemade chips.

"You seriously didn't let them eat?"

Deacon curled his arm over my chest and kissed my temple again. "You get first choice." He moved over to get a plate and passed it to me, not knowing I was melting on the inside.

How the fuck did I get so lucky?

Please don't take this from me.

Using the utensils, I picked out my food and waited for Deacon to take his. We went to the dining table and sat. Riker and Nox followed. Riker already gulped down food, while Nox ate slower and grumpier.

This was my new family.

My life was looking up because of the man sitting close to my side.

It didn't matter what he did for a living. Nothing mattered but capturing and keeping this happiness buzzing through me; it was my new addiction. Deacon was a drug I wanted to get high from every day.

At least it was a healthier obsession.

I just had to make sure I got to keep him.

"So," Riker drew out. "How are you handling knowing about shifters?" He sat back and rubbed at his stomach before leaning forward to take another forkful.

"I haven't had a breakdown, which has me thinking I'm doing well."

Riker cackled. "You're funny."

"We're sitting down with Santiago tomorrow," Nox announced.

Instinctively, I placed my hand over Deacon's, just as he parted his lips to speak, and squeezed. He glanced at me, and I smiled.

"It's okay." I looked back to Nox. "I haven't forgotten your jobs, and I understand why you want to do it so soon. I once overheard his shipment of drugs arrives every last week in the month. Which means it'll be on the streets by the weekend."

Nox nodded.

"Makes sense you guys want to stop that."

Nox leaned back in his seat. "You have no feelings for your father?"

"None."

"Then there'll be no judgment down the track toward Deacon for doing this?"

"Nox," Deacon started, but went quiet when I tapped two fingers on his hand.

"There won't be. Santiago is an evil man. He's made many lives miserable. I may not want to know the details of what happens, but his life ending won't be a loss."

Nox's gaze shifted to Deacon, and he nodded once before he stood and left with his empty plate.

"That's good, then," Riker announced with a big smile.

"What?" I asked.

Deacon curled an arm around my shoulders and drew me into him to kiss the top of my head. "Nox accepts you into the family."

Riker nodded. "Not that it mattered if he didn't because Deacon would want you anyway. Man, you two look cute together. I want a fated mate," he whined.

Deacon chuckled. "One day, Riker."

He beamed. "I hope so."

As Riker spoke to Deacon, I tuned them out as my gut clenched over the thought of Deacon walking into danger tomorrow night.

He could get hurt, or worse.

The meal I just ate threatened to rise.

Tipping my head to the side and back, I watched as Deacon talked. He already had me addicted, and if he got injured.... A shudder ran over my body.

"Leave us," I heard Deacon order.

Riker left without a sound, so I presumed that whatever he saw or scented made him see it wasn't the time to argue with the bear.

"Rio, what's wrong?"

Turning into him, I pushed at his chest until he scooted his chair back. I slipped onto his lap and buried my face into his neck.

"What's wrong, love?" Deacon asked softly.

Love.

My heart skipped a beat. "Tomorrow night."

He stiffened. "Are you actually upset about Santiago?"

"No." *You big fool.* "I'm being selfish. In one day, you've given me a taste of a good life, and I don't want to imagine my days without you."

His body relaxed as he wrapped me up in his arms. "Nothing will happen to me, Rio."

I didn't want to be called Rio. *Love.* I was even greedy about wanting to hear the endearment all the time.

This man was wrecking me, but I wouldn't have it any other way. This was so different to what Mamá had with Santiago. This went both ways. I wasn't in this alone. Deacon was with me all the way.

"Promise me," I demanded.

"I promise."

Promises could be broken. A link couldn't, though. If anything happened to Deacon, I would feel it through a bond, Ruth had told me so. I could get to him, help him. I'd also asked Ruth how the connection between fated mates was finalized.

My body trembled, my dick jerked, and my stomach fluttered as I pulled back and met his gaze. "Take me to bed, Deacon. Fuck me and bite me."

His pupils blew wide and a growl rumbled out. Through it, he said, "We don't have to—"

I rested my hand over his mouth.

The sweet bear was always trying to make me comfortable. Didn't want to pressure me.

He didn't understand I'd already made the choice to accept him in all ways and that meant to finalize the connection between us. He wasn't getting rid of me, and I didn't want to give him up.

This was forever.

Dropping my hand, I kissed his jaw. "I want to. I need to. Fate saw us joined and it's only taken me hours to know they made the right choice." Sliding my hands up his chest, I leaned into him. "You want me, yes?"

"Always."

"I want you and that won't change, no matter how much time we spend getting to know each other more. You've blindly accepted me because this fated mate business isn't to be messed with. We can bind together and then get to know one another. I see no reason to wait when all I'll ever want is to be at your side."

He cupped my cheeks and intently looked into my eyes. I caught his animal flash in them before he said, "You'll never regret your choice in me, love."

"I know I won't." I dipped in and pressed my lips to his, and against them I muttered, "Bed."

CHAPTER TWELVE

DEACON

I stood with Rio in my arms and stalked from the dining room. Racing up the stairs, we entered my bedroom where I kicked the door closed.

Breathing unsteadily, I reminded myself I had to calm down.

This was my mate's first time, and I'd make sure he enjoyed every fucking moment of it.

Placing Rio on his feet, I pinched his chin and tipped his head back, claiming his lips in a hot, wet kiss of tongue, lips, and teeth.

My cock goddamn throbbed behind my pants. I placed my hands on his hips, drawing them in against mine to grind our erections together.

Rio moaned into my mouth.

He was mine.

All fucking mine.

My mate. My *fated* mate. Mine forever. He'd accepted me. He wanted me to fuck and bite him, connecting us for the rest of our lives.

Fuck.

Christ.

I had to make this good for him. I had to show him how damn important he was.

My bear chuffed inside, already content that I was pleasing him—if my mate's whimpering, needy sounds were to go by. The animal was happy we were already pleasing him, touching him, and about to make him ours.

Rio broke away from my mouth to pant and stared up at me with such unhidden desire and need, it rocked me. Had my gut swirling and cock aching.

He licked his red, swollen lips. "I-I want you in me."

A punch of arousal had me sucking in a sharp breath.

He looked drunk on lust.

"Anything you want, love."

Anything.

I gripped the bottom of his tee and slowly drew it up. He lifted his arms, and I slid it from his body, throwing it to the floor. Rio did the same to me but laid a kiss on my naked chest after.

I watched on as he stepped back to remove his shoes, socks, pants, and underwear. Unable to look away while he revealed his whole body, my cock jerked. I wanted to mark his skin all over.

My mouth watered from the thought of getting my mouth and teeth into his flesh. I knew he'd make sounds, like he had when we'd kissed, but more so because I wanted to do it as I stretched his hole for my taking.

Rio backed up, panting, and stopped when the backs of his legs touched the bed. He licked his lips, eyes roaming over me. "Show me all of you, Deacon."

I took off my shoes and socks. My button flew with a pop and the zipper broke when I tore them open, eager to get my pants down to give my mate what he wanted.

I gripped my dick and ran my palm up and down as I stalked slowly closer. Rio climbed onto the bed.

"Back. Spread your legs, love. I'll fuck you with my tongue first to get you ready."

His dick twitched at my words. Rio fell back onto his ass and then down to his back. A deep red coated his cheeks when he spread his legs wide for me.

Mine.

Kneeling on the bed, I crawled between his legs and slipped down to my elbows. I nipped at his inner thighs, which had him gasping and crying out.

He quivered, running his hands up and down over his stomach. I kissed where I'd had my teeth in and then licked there before I dragged my tongue up. I glided my hands under him, lifted his hips, and buried my face and mouth into his ass. On the first lick, he yelled my name. On the second, he squirmed on the bed, and the third, when I stuck my tongue deeper and harder into his hole, my mate, *my* Rio, clawed at the sheets, moaning.

Hearing his noises and seeing the way his body reacted was heady. My cock leaked onto the sheets. I rutted my hips into the bed, looking for friction as pleasure from watching Rio had my body tightening.

Pulling my mouth off, I licked up to his balls and sucked gently on one as I slipped a finger into his wet hole to run over his prostate.

"Holy fuck," he yelled, peering down at me with a glassy stare and flushed cheeks, biting his bottom lip.

"More?" I asked, voice rough.

He nodded, planting his feet into the bed to push down on my finger. "Please."

I added another as I dribbled more spit to his glistening hole. He moaned and rocked up and down.

"Deacon... Deacon."

"Soon," I told him gruffly, bear riding my tone. As I fucked him with my fingers at a gentle pace, I got to my knees and reached over to the bedside table to grab the lube.

Opening it, I squirted some onto my fingers and rubbed them around his hole, adding another finger.

He arched, mouth opening and closing. He gripped his own dick and squeezed. I tapped it away with my free hand and shook my head. "Not yet."

"I need, Deacon. I need you in me."

"Soon, mate."

"Please, *please*."

"Soon."

I planted my free hand down beside his head and loomed over him as I fucked my fingers inside him, stretching. He grabbed my arm, rocking down on my digits, but my sneaky mate used his other hand to wind it around my leaking, aching cock.

"*Please*," he begged.

"Fuck," I clipped, removing my fingers. "Roll over, mate, to your knees."

Rio shivered, but managed to do as I said, jutting his ass up and back. Offering me his slicked hole for the taking, and Christ, I looked forward to making it mine.

Leaning down, I kissed his spine and ran my hands over his ass cheeks. Lightly slapping, which had my mate moaning and pushing against my hands.

He rested his upper body down to the bed, looking back to me, licking his lips before biting down on his bottom one. I inserted my thumb into his hole and out again, watching his dazed gaze drift off. I held my pulsing cock and pressed the tip to his wetness.

My mate's body was smaller than mine. Something I fucking loved. Made it easier to touch my hands down to the bed at each side of him so I could slowly feed my dick into his strangling heat.

"Oh God. Oh hell," Rio chanted, trying to push back faster. I gripped one hip and held him still.

"Slow, love," I ordered.

"No. please. Want you all the way in. Fill me."

Christ, he looked drugged on the feeling of me being in him.

I ground my teeth together to stop myself from thrusting in and hurting him. He still needed to get used to me.

"Yes," he breathed when I was finally all the way in.

My labored breaths brushed over his neck. "Mate," I groaned as he tightened around me even more.

Pulling out, I thrust back in.

"Fuck yes," Rio cried, fingers digging into the bed.

I bucked my hips back and forth, driving my hard and throbbing cock into his waiting and stretched warmth.

I went back and forth, fast and unsteady, out of control.

I fucked my mate.

Made him mine.

And when his hand slid between himself and the bed, I curled an arm across his chest and pulled him back into my chest. His hand circled his cock and he tugged. I licked over his neck, nipped, and listened to his heavy breathing, felt his trembling body.

"Deacon," he whimpered when his hand lost the rhythm.

As both of us drew closer to the teasing edge, I sucked on Rio's shoulder and then brought my teeth down upon it. They lengthened against his damp, flushed skin before I bit.

Rio threw his head back into my shoulder and cried out, coming all over the sheets while I emptied myself inside of his gripping warmth.

The bond clicked into place inside my chest, right around my fast-beating heart, where it always belonged. Now we would be able to get a rough sense of each other's emotions and know if either of us were in danger. Rio would also stop aging rapidly like all humans and take on the slower rate we shifters did. Meaning we would have many more decades together. This was all information I would soon tell my beautiful fated mate.

Rio gasped, touching his chest. I withdrew my teeth, and they reshaped to my human ones. My chest expanded; pride swept over me at seeing my mark on him.

Slowly, I pulled out of my mate, causing him to shudder. I lay on the bed, dragging his pliant body over mine as he caught his breath. A lazy smile graced his lips.

"I feel you," he whispered, mouthing at my collarbone.

"Mine," I bit out.

He patted my stomach. "Yes, and you're mine." His smile grew when he touched the mark on his shoulder. He seemed very satisfied with himself.

Elation turned my stomach on itself.

My mate was happy.

Christ, I wanted to embed my cock inside him again already. I wanted him stinking of my cum and sweat.

Rolling us, I kissed and nipped at his lips. He mewed around my attacks and wrapped his arms around me. His cock twitched. Mine jerked. Both slowly fattening.

He'd be sore, though.

I ran a hand down his side as I sucked at his tongue. Slipping a hand between his legs, I pressed at his dripping hole. He squirmed, gasped, and hooked one leg over me, giving me access.

Fuck.

"We shouldn't," I said against his lips. "You'll be sore."

"Deacon, I want to go again." He rubbed his cock into me.

"Later, after—" I groaned when he snuck a hand between us and gripped me. "Love," I warned.

He pushed his hips up and slid back down with me in his still loosened hole.

"Yes," he breathed, closing his eyes and grinning. He

tried to hide the delight of getting his way by biting his bottom lip, but it still swam in his eyes.

Fuck, it was going to be hard to deny my mate.

"I like the feel of you in me," he admitted, face flushing.

A growl rumbled out. I jutted my hips forward. "I like being inside you, mate."

I rolled us so I lay on the bed. Rio pressed his hands to my chest and sat back on me. He released a moan and squeezed himself around my cock.

I'd never get enough of him.

Jesus, he looked like a fucking angel as he shifted up and down on me, fucking himself.

I'd please him any time he wanted. I'd do anything for him.

His head rolled back as he groaned, bouncing on me, and I knew he was hitting the right spot inside him when his fingers dug into my skin, and he tightened around me even more.

Fuck.

Christ.

My balls drew up at his blissed-out expression with hooded eyes and a curve to his lips.

"Deacon," he cried as he came over my stomach and chest.

I grabbed his hips and thrust up a few more times before I unloaded and saturated his walls.

CHAPTER THIRTEEN

RIO

*W*e'd only just entered the kitchen the next morning when Deacon's phone rang, and he excused himself with a kiss to my forehead to take the call. I went over to the coffee machine with a soft smile as I thought back to the night before. Yes, I was sore, but surprisingly, I liked the feeling.

Turning from pouring a coffee, I stole a croissant from the box on the counter on the way to the refrigerator to grab some cream, when Riker suddenly appeared.

"Jesus," I yelled, pressing a hand to my racing heart.

He had his hands clasped in front of him and danced from one foot to another.

Shaking my head, I sighed. "Go ahead and say it before Deacon gets back."

He moved around me. "Can I see the claiming bite? Did you like it with him? That was your first time, right? Did he fuck you? I can't image Deacon taking it up the—"

"Riker," I called, reaching out to grab his arm.

He stilled under my hold.

I dropped my hand and shifted the tee I borrowed from Deacon to the side. Riker whistled and wiggled.

I couldn't help but smile at him. He was such an exuberant shifter, it was hard to be annoyed or angry with him and all his questions. Hell, I just wanted to hug the guy.

Leaning in, I whispered, "It was my first time. I did like it with him, and I can't wait to do it again. Deacon took care of *me* in all ways."

He silently clapped. "Welcome to the family."

Warmth spread through my chest.

Family.

My own special family.

Stepping toward him, I gave Riker a quick hug. "Thank you."

His eyes flared before they softened. He reached up and patted me on the head. "You're welcome." He glanced behind me. "He hugged me," he yelled before running from the room.

It was hard to believe Riker was a killer or that he'd gone through such a vile past to begin with. One that Deacon and Nox suffered from also because of their previous packs.

Last night, Deacon had told me about some of their history as we lay in the bath together. If their pack hadn't already been taken care of, I would have found a way to deal with them. I'd been so angry, I even considered using Santiago's resources until Deacon reminded me it was a long time ago and it had been sorted by them and their animals. But their tormented pasts were the main reason for them to have the jobs they did.

An arm curled around my chest, and I was brought back against heat. Plump lips touched my temple and a content noise fell from my lips as I tipped my neck to the side, knowing what Deacon wanted.

He dipped down and pressed another soft kiss to his claiming bite. He'd been paying a lot of attention to it this morning. From a gentle swipe of his finger, a lick of his tongue, or a brush of his lips.

"You confiding in him would have meant the world. Thank you."

Turning in his arm, I wrapped mine around his waist. Not that my hands reached because of his wide form.

I looked up at him. "You don't need to thank me. We're all family now."

"We are. Speaking of family. Ruth is on the way over with your mother." His jaw clenched.

"Is everything okay?"

"Yes. Your mother wants to speak with you."

"Wait, she's awake and sober? Ruth's a miracle worker if that's the case."

There was another clench of his jaw. I knew what his irritation was about—how she'd turned up to Santiago's the other night, which caused trouble for me.

If the shoe was on the other foot, I would be pissed too, because our lives had been on the line.

I swiped at the line between his brows. "I'm not going to forgive her easily, Deacon."

He grunted. "Good. She doesn't deserve your forgiveness, mate. I know it's not the first time she's put your lives at risk with that man. I won't ever trust her, but for you, she can come here and have her words."

Nodding, I hugged him close. "That's fair."

And it was because now I didn't just have myself to think of.

I SAT on the couch in the living room with Deacon standing at my back. He'd just slipped his phone back in his pocket after texting Ruth where we'd be waiting in the house.

Reaching for his hand on my shoulder, I asked again, "Are you sure you won't sit down?"

Deacon's gaze didn't leave the doorway. "My bear is on edge right now. I'll stay at your back." I knew he left off "guarding it."

I wasn't sure why his bear felt uneasy; it was only my mamá.

Hearing their footsteps, I glanced to the door as they stepped into the room. Ruth was first, and I expected her to at least look at us, but she marched in and over to the chair by the window and sat. My gut swarm with uncertainty. I peered over to see a very tired-looking Mamá. She paused to stare at me, clutching her bag to her stomach.

"Mamá, would you like to sit?"

She nodded and moved over to the couch opposite me, taking a seat with her bag on her lap instead of putting it on the coffee table that sat between us. Mamá flicked her attention to Deacon before it landed on me with a tight smile.

"How are you this morning?" I asked.

"I've been better," she admitted. Which was understandable since she hadn't had a drink or taken any drugs to get through the day. At least her eyes seemed clear.

We all looked to the entryway that led into the kitchen where Nox and Riker had just walked in. Had Deacon texted them? Nox went behind the couch to stand at Deacon's side with his arms crossed over his chest. While Riker surprised me by laying on my couch with his head on my lap.

I grinned down at him before reaching back for Deacon's hand again. "Mamá. I'd like you to meet Ruth's sons, Deacon, Nox, and Riker."

"She told me about them." Her tone held judgment as her gaze flicked to Deacon again.

It had me stiffening in annoyance. Had she already formed an opinion of them?

"So, you know Deacon and I are..." *Shit, how do I explain our bond*? "...getting married?" I blurted. That would at least tell her how serious I was about the man behind me.

Her lips thinned and she glared. "Married? To a man?"

The disgust in her voice had me jerking my head back in shock. We'd never spoken of our thoughts about people's sexuality, but I presumed she wasn't a bigot since she'd never said anything bad.

"What did you come here to discuss?" Nox asked.

I held my hand up. "He makes me happy, Mamá."

Didn't she at least want that for me?

She scoffed. "I don't want to speak of your... whatever it will be between you two."

I glanced at Ruth who gave me a small, sad smile.

Dread coursed through me.

I should have known. I shouldn't have expected anything better. This was the woman who chose to use substances to numb her life because her husband grew bored of her. She never cared she had a child to look after.

Her wants and needs were always more important. I was stupid for even thinking she would change after one night with another mother who was good to her children.

She was never a mother. I'd coddled her and her actions, holding out hope she would snap out of her dedication to a man who used and abused her.

But I should have realized that she never would. She didn't want to be a mother. She hadn't wanted to raise me. All she ever wanted was a life with a man who didn't love her.

I'd always been nothing to her. Accepting the knowledge crushed my soul a little, but at least I had people who would support me. People who loved me.

She now had no one.

Honestly, I felt sorry for the woman who birthed me. She'd never be called Mamá again; she didn't deserve such a title. From now on, she'd be known by her Christian name: Isabella.

Deacon rubbed circles into my shoulder and Riker reached up and patted the hand I had on his arm. I hadn't even realized I'd been gripping him in frustration.

Swallowing thickly, I asked, "What *did* you come here for, then?"

"To tell you what a disappointment of a child you are. You disgraced me by bringing a stranger into the house that tried to pick apart my life, my past." She laughed humorlessly. "You disgraced your father by being a failure and now by taking a man as a partner. My life would have been so much better if I'd got rid of you before you were born." Shaking her head, she slid her hand into her bag. "But I can do something now. For me. For Luis."

Just as I saw her pull a gun out, Riker rolled, flicking his wrist. Isabella screamed. Deacon let out a roar while he shifted. I was lifted off the couch and covered by a large body.

In a matter of seconds, I peeked out from under Nox to see Ruth holding Isabella by the throat. With fear in her wide gaze, she dangled, clawing at Ruth's hand.

I glanced down, noticing a blade sticking out of her knee before moving my attention to the side where Riker crouched with a silent snarl on his face.

Deacon stood on his hind legs, only to bend, and flip the couch out of the way.

"Deacon, no," Ruth ordered. "You don't want to be the one to deal with her. Think of your mate."

His bear landed on all fours and snapped a huge paw forward, shattering the wooden coffee table. Tears streamed down Isabella's face as she stared at Deacon in pure horror.

Ruth lowered her enough for her feet to touch the ground and lessened her hold on her neck. She coughed and gasped.

I tapped at Nox's arm. He pulled back, stood, and picked me up, but ushered me behind his back.

My mate paced in front of Isabella, growling low.

He was beyond pissed.

I should have been too. But I was more stunned that she tried to kill me in front of witnesses. What had she really been thinking?

"I don't get it," I mumbled. Nox glanced over his shoulder to me. "Why would she even try to kill me here in front of people?"

Nox grunted and looked back to the others. "Answer him," he ordered darkly.

I moved to the side slightly to see that Isabella was already looking over here.

When Ruth released her, she swayed and winced, trying to back away from the noisy bear.

"Move again and I'll stick another knife in you," Riker warned.

She stilled. Her breaths were choppy. "For Luis. He'd welcome me back if I killed you."

A strangled noise dropped from me. "Is this what he told you or what you've thought?"

Her gaze narrowed and she said nothing.

It was only what she thought.

Pathetic.

Deacon roared, lunging at her. She screamed, falling to her ass, and retreating until her back hit the wall.

"H-He's a monster and you're with him. You—"

"No," I snapped, and she clamped her lips closed.

Satisfaction filled me. I'd never stood up to her before. Always let her say and do anything she wanted. But I wouldn't any longer. She was nothing to me now or ever again. I had my family.

"You don't get to say anything about him or me anymore. I should have stood up to you a long time ago, but I'd always hoped you'd wake up. You won't. You're sick and I doubt you'll ever get better." I glanced to Ruth. "Do we call the police?"

Ruth shook her head. "I'll arrange for people to come get her. She'll be dealt with under shifter laws because she risked a fated mate's life. I'm sorry, Rio and Deacon. I could scent the weapon on her—" Deacon snarled at Ruth. She bared her neck to him. "I knew from trying to speak with her that she wasn't taking in anything I said and instead had come up with her own plan. One I knew we could deal with together. I also thought you, Rio, needed to witness your mother for who she truly is."

Sick and twisted in a way that whatever came to her, she deserved.

Ruth had made the right choice. I offered her a reassuring smile and nodded, then looked back to Isabella.

I walked over to Deacon who stopped at my side, and I ran my fingers through his fur. "I want you to look at the people around you, but especially the bear, *my* bear. I want you to know that I've never been as happy and felt as loved as I do from these people—in just two days—than I've ever felt before. I'm going to have an amazing future. One filled with so much love. But know that this will be the last time I see you. I don't want anything to do with you again. Goodbye, Isabella."

Deacon followed me as I walked from the room with my head held high, and for the first time, without guilt in my heart.

CHAPTER FOURTEEN

DEACON

*M*y bear and I didn't like leaving our mate after what happened with his soon-to-be dead mother. But we also wanted this matter dealt with, so it didn't become a bigger problem for our future. Which was why, after Ruth promised with her life that she would protect him, and I called in some human hired help to guard outside, I left Rio curled up under a blanket on the couch while Ruth doted on him as they watched a movie.

My brothers and I stood outside the same restaurant from a couple of nights ago. It was hard to believe that I'd known my mate for such a short amount of time; it felt so much longer.

Smiling faintly, I rubbed at my chest, feeling the connection in there.

PROTECTED BY THE BEAR SHIFTER

I made a promise to come home later to Rio and I would make sure I kept it.

"Let's get this done," I said, opening the door.

The same waitress led us back to the meeting room and left. I entered first, seeing Santiago smirking from where he sat on the other side of the table. Amusement already gleamed in his gaze.

Riker slipped over to the left side of the room, Nox the right. They knew their jobs. Just like the men we had outside would take care of Santiago's people before they entered the restaurant, and others would get the innocent employees out before they locked the front down and left.

While we took care of business in the back here.

Santiago watched my brothers, his smirk dimming, before he glanced to his right-hand man, who got out his phone and texted something. Santiago's attention shot back to me as I approached.

"What is your offer?" Santiago asked.

"I don't have one," I said, stopping at the other side of the table.

This man was my kill.

My bear needed it.

I needed it.

We wanted his blood on our hands because it meant our mate would be safe. The man who made his life hell would be dead, and Rio could move on from the years that had caused him nothing but pain and trouble.

Then we'd slaughter anyone who didn't bow to our changes. Who could cause problems for Rio. Anyone who was devoted to Santiago.

Santiago laughed. The men around him joined in.

The door behind me opened and surprise flickered through Santiago's eyes when I didn't turn to see his men pouring in.

Let them come. We'd take them all on.

"What do you mean?" Santiago demanded. I didn't miss his hand sliding under the table.

"You should have taken the original offer. That was your first mistake—"

"Watch your tone, boy."

Riker cackled off to the side, but Santiago didn't look away from me as his jaw clenched.

"Whatever you think you've planned, think again," he warned. "You either walk away with your life indebted to me, or you don't walk away and end up in body bags. Those are the only choices you have."

"Choices." I nodded, humming under my breath, and then said to the room, "I'll give my own now. All of you who work for Santiago, this will be your only choice. Walk now and live. Stay at his side and die."

Santiago spluttered, pushed his chair back, and stood, pointing his gun at my face. "Who the fuck do you think you are?"

I grinned. "Before things happen, I want you to know Rio will live a safe and happy life with me."

He spat off to the side, spewing something in Spanish. "He is no son of mine."

Disgust had my upper lip rising and my hands fisting at my sides.

Rio has a better life now, I reminded myself.

Not a day would go by without Rio smiling. He

deserved that and so much more after having to put up with this man and his mother.

"Deacon," Riker whined, wanting permission to attack.

"Soon," I told him.

I heard him clap in excitement.

Rio wouldn't want us to slaughter everyone without giving them a second chance to walk, since Santiago had interrupted the first one.

"Men—"

I clicked and then held my hand up at Santiago.

His eyes bulged and he went to spew more shit, but I allowed my bear to appear in my gaze and voice when I rumbled, "Silence."

Santiago took a step back, his hand shaking. "*Diablo*," he whispered.

I turned my head to the side and said, "One last chance for everyone, but Santiago. Walk now and you won't die. But if you stupidly wish to avenge this man in the future, think again." I licked over my teeth as they lengthened. A growl rolled over every next word I said. "I. Won't. Allow. It."

Riker's fox chittered from inside him.

Nox's tiger snarled low, vibrating his chest.

About twenty men headed out the door. If they made speculations over what they saw or heard, no one would believe them. The fear I could taste in the air had me thinking they wouldn't talk. Besides, it wasn't like we shifted in front of them, and in the end, there wouldn't be any proof of what happened anyway.

All evidence would incinerate after we were done.

"Come back," Santiago yelled. His panic saturated the room as he screamed something in Spanish.

The scent of fear spiked higher, not only from his men, but Santiago as well.

Knowing he was scared had my bear and me chuffing in glee.

Yet, no one else ran.

I wanted to laugh if they thought my brothers and I weren't scarier than Santiago.

They'd soon seen.

"Shoot," Santiago ordered.

"Now," I roared, flinging my hands out to my sides as my claws grew and sharpened. I dodged to the right as he fired. The bullet sailed over my head.

More shots were fired.

Some from his men, others from my brothers.

People screamed. Some cried. And others died.

I jumped, sliding over the table to land beside Santiago and his right-hand man. Their guns were trained on me as I stood from my crouch. Their gazes were wide and terrified as my bones popped and shifted.

Urine stank up the room.

Their fingers got trigger happy. Two landed in me, but we dodged the rest and swiped at their legs, stomach, and chest. Chomping down on an arm, while we stood on the other body. Bones broke. Blood sprayed.

And their cries were music to our ears.

We left them bleeding, knowing they were injured enough they couldn't move, and went to help our brothers.

Begging started, but it was too late for them.

Someone foolishly yelled their attack and landed on my back. We reached up with a paw and pulled them off, taking their neck in our mouth and snapping it with one bite.

There was more blood, more cries, and dying by claws and teeth.

The fox raced by chittering and launched onto someone's back, nipping at their neck, crawling over and around them, biting in all places they touched before bouncing off the falling dead and onto the next.

As we charged a new target and barreled into them, we saw Nox, still in human form, stab one in the neck and twist to knife another in the gut.

Death drenched our senses.

We went to our hind legs and roared.

The men who still stood, dropped to their knees, giving in. The tiger and fox took them out while we went back over to Santiago.

He lay on the floor, clutching his stomach and neck.

The shift back took seconds.

Naked, I crouched beside him and grinned.

"As I said, your first mistake was not taking our offer. The second, and worst, the one that sealed your death, was how you've treated my mate his whole life." Leaning in, I wrapped my hand around his throat. His hands slapped at mine and tried to pull it away. "Die, knowing your son will live on happy and loves getting fucked by me."

I tightened my grip, watching his face redden, his eyes bulge, and his mouth open and close like a fish out of water as his life drained from his body.

When his arms flopped to the floor, I stood over him as Nox stopped beside me. He aimed his gun and fired a shot between Santiago's eyes.

I lifted my head and glanced around the room, seeing that bodies practically covered the floor.

It was done.

Santiago wouldn't be a problem any longer.

I hoped he was already burning in hell and remembering what I said to him; the knowledge of his son being mine would have cut him deeper than anything else. He was a petty, stupid, bigoted man after all.

"Ready?" I asked.

Nox nodded. "Riker," he called, and the fox came running. He licked at his bloody teeth before he shifted and danced around us.

"Did you see my move? Did you see it? I was awesome." He shook his arms out, rolled his shoulders. "Man, it's been too long since I killed. I missed it." He bounced. "When can we do it again?"

"When we get a job."

"Unless someone pisses us off, right? Can I take Rio out to a club, and then I know you'll get pissed at guys who look at him—"

"Riker," I clipped. "Find some clothes."

He sighed. "Fine."

I took some clothes off a guy my size, one that didn't have as much blood on the fabric, and got dressed. Thankfully my injuries had already healed from shifting or I'd get an earful from Rio. I didn't want him worrying either.

We walked out the back and waited.

Dashiell, who we called Dash, walked down the

alleyway with the grace of all elves. While Soren, the only vampire we associated with, appeared in front of us.

"Did you get them all?" I asked Soren. We'd paid him well to wipe the minds of all employees our human security team got out.

He rolled his eyes and looked at his fingernails. "Why do you question my ability?"

Smirking, I shrugged. "Because you get pouty when I do."

He flashed his fangs as he hissed, "I do not."

"Is it true?" Dash asked, stopping beside Soren.

Faking ignorance, I asked, "What?"

"Yes!" Riker yelled. "Deacon has a fated mate, isn't that awesome?"

Soren reached out and ran a hand over Riker's orange hair. "It gives us hope, sweetheart, because if your brute of a brother found one, then we can too."

Riker clapped. "I know."

"Speaking of, I have to get back to him," I said.

"They're sickly sweet, but it's cute," Riker told them.

I shoved at him and asked Dash, "You've got the rest?"

"No one will be found." He held up his hand and fire lit over it.

"Thanks. We'll be in touch."

"Good luck with your fated," Dash said, as Soren disappeared.

Smiling, I nodded my thanks.

Not that I needed luck. I already had it when Rio entered my world, and I would have it for the rest of our lives as he'd be at my side.

I hoped Dash and Soren did find their fated. I wasn't the only one who deserved to be this fucking content.

Need flashed through me to get home faster, wanting my mate in my arms.

CHAPTER FIFTEEN

RIO

It was strange being in class after a few weeks of being at home with Deacon. In Deacon's presence all the time. Having had him all over me every chance we got. I rubbed a hand over my face, averting my train of thought before it got carried away. Which was easy to do when it came to Deacon since I was completely besotted by him.

In the weeks after Santiago was... taken care of, I'd been visited by some detectives to ask me questions about the explosion at the business in what they believed took the life of Santiago. They didn't seem too cut-up over it, which was understandable. Of course, I informed them I knew nothing and had been home all night with Deacon and his family, and they all confirmed my story. The detectives then queried if I knew the whereabouts of Isabella.

When I told them no, they mentioned they found evidence she'd left town to go to Mexico.

"It wouldn't surprise me. She's always been... heart-broken by Santiago's mistreatment. I tried to help her, but nothing I did worked. So, I hope this trip will be good for her."

They'd shared a look before nodding and leaving, but that was after letting me know I wasn't a suspect in the explosion. Still, they didn't want me to leave town in case they had more questions.

So far, they hadn't been back.

The only other person I heard from was a lawyer, who told me a piece of information that shocked the hell out of me. Santiago had left me one million dollars. I didn't know what happened to all his other fortune and I didn't care. I didn't even want that money since it came from that man.

Deacon told me I wouldn't need it. I'd never need for anything from that life. I had a new one. A brighter, safer, loved one. Besides, I still had my own money.

Which was the reason why I donated his money to Save the Children charity. If I could help any child in any way, I wanted to, because I'd been saved.

Sighing, I leaned back on my seat and tapped my pen to the table. Really, what was I even doing here? Why did I come back? I never wanted a business degree. It was what Santiago forced upon me. Yes, I liked learning, but I also held a secret passion for cooking. Something I only explored when I could at home and after taking care of *that* woman. It was never often, though, but now it could be.

I already knew Deacon would support anything I chose to do.

So, I didn't have to be in the class. I didn't have to stay on this degree. I had the choice of doing whatever I wanted.

Hell, I wished I realized this before I sat through the previous class.

It didn't matter, though. I was heading home to Deacon.

Home.

A giddy rush prickled under my skin.

Smiling, I packed up my things.

"What are you doing?" Nox asked.

I'd forgotten he was on Rio duty that day. Apparently being a fated mate entailed bodyguards whenever I was apart from Deacon and out on my own. I wasn't sure if it was just a possessive shifter thing or if it happened with all species.

No matter. I didn't mind having a security detail if it meant Deacon would worry less and he could get work done. I didn't realize that as well as working for their government, they also had businesses to manage. They had employees but involved themselves a lot as well, working from one of the tallest buildings in the middle of the city.

"I'm quitting this degree and looking at a cooking course or something."

He blinked. "Cooking?"

"That's right." I grinned.

Nox sighed, but stood, waiting for me. He was still a prickly tiger shifter, but that was just him, and I didn't take offense to his glare or clenched jaw. He could be annoyed all he wanted; it wasn't going to bother me, not when deep down, he cared for his brother's mate.

I slung my backpack over my shoulder and started down the steps, hoping to get out of here before the professor arrived.

Just as we neared the door, it opened and in tripped my usual professor, Kieran Higgins. My peers chuckled as Higgins blushed and pushed his glasses up.

When he saw Nox and me standing near, he jumped in surprise.

"Sorry, professor. I have an emergency to get to," I told him.

"O-Okay." He nodded, clutching his briefcase to his chest. He cleared his throat and started for his desk. "I would like—"

People snickered, and I glanced back to see Higgins stumbling forward. He must have tripped from his shoelace being untied because he quickly crouched to do it up.

I winced in sympathy for him. Professor Higgins had always been easy to read that attention on him made him nervous. I'd often wondered why he picked this job in the first place. Maybe to challenge himself?

Shaking my head, I went to walk out the door, but my gaze stopped on Nox, who looked frozen. He stared at the floor with his hands clenching and unclenching at his sides.

"Nox?"

His brows bunched up, and he took a wooden step toward me but stopped.

PROTECTED BY THE BEAR SHIFTER

What was wrong with him?

Just when I was about to call out to him again, he walked my way and out the door before me, stalking down the hallway.

Okay, that was strange.

Closing the door after me, I heard Higgins restart the class. I'd email the dean and let him know my plans. Once I figured them out myself.

When I caught up to Nox in the hallway, I asked, "Are you okay?"

"Fine," he bit out through clenched teeth.

"Are you sure?"

"Yes," he hissed.

"You know I'm an okay person to talk to. If something's on your mind, I can help."

"No," he stated, and after a pause, he added tightly, "Thank you."

I hid my smile behind my hand. "No problem." It didn't surprise me Nox didn't want to open up. Still, I'd mention his tension to Deacon and get him to check on his brother.

By the time we pulled into the garage, I'd lost count of the times I thought the car was going to break when Nox strangled the steering wheel and it creaked.

"Deacon's home. I'm going into the office to make sure Riker didn't burn it down."

It was the most he'd ever said to me. I nodded mutely as I exited the car, worried if I commented, he wouldn't do it again.

The garage door connecting to the house opened.

I turned to my bear and said, "I'm quitting my busi-

141

ness degree and looking at something in cooking. Also, there's something on your brother's mind, so you might want to check in with him."

Deacon nodded as he approached. "I will, and you know I'll stand by you with whatever you want to do."

Desire twisted my gut. I ran and jumped. Deacon grabbed me with a grin as I wrapped my arms and legs around him.

"I know, because I'm the luckiest guy in the world."

"No, love, I am."

"Deacon."

His lips twitched. "Yes?"

"No one's home but us, right?"

His nostrils flared; his gaze darkened after taking in my arousal that rolled through me and made me squirm on the inside. "Right," he growled.

I grinned and climbed down from him. "Good. Stay here, please. Count slowly to one hundred, and then, my bear, come and hunt me down."

His chest rumbled at the idea, and his cock thickened under his jeans.

Laughing, I ran to the door, still listening to the rumble of his beast continuing.

An excited thrill swept down my spine and had my dick throbbing. I clenched my ass and bit down on my bottom lip to keep from moaning. I had to be extra quiet. I just hoped I could, wanting to be ready when he found me.

I sped through the house like my feet were on fire and skidded into our bedroom where I got undressed and grabbed the lube. In record time, I oiled up, stretched myself, and made another mad dash to hide.

Just as I was running down the hall to my destination of the movie room, I heard the deep voice of Deacon and his bear combined, "I can hear you, mate."

My pulse ticked up as I rounded another corner and sped to the dark room. I closed the door after me, pitching into blackness. Silently, I cursed myself, but I felt my way over to the walk-in storage closet in the corner. I opened that door and closed it after me.

A hiss escaped when I kicked something.

Shit, shit, shit. He probably heard that.

My heart flew franticly behind my ribs, and I nearly let out a laugh when I realized I'd been running around the house with a hard-on slapping up and down—which he also could have heard—while I waited for my man to come find and fuck me.

Yet, the excitement of it all was like an injection of adrenaline and desire into my veins.

I slipped into the corner where the shelf would cover my body if he opened the door and turned on the light. I pressed a hand to my chest and breathed slowly, but deep.

A shudder danced over me as I reached around and ran some fingers over my hole. I bit my bottom lip, to keep my sounds inside, and pushed my digits into me. Stretching myself, I gripped the shelf and closed my eyes.

My dick jerked and ached, wanting attention, but I wouldn't give it; the excitement would have me coming too quickly, and I wanted to save it for Deacon.

Heavy footsteps reverberated in the movie room. I stilled, then slowly pulled my fingers free.

I trembled from the anticipation.

The door crashed open and light streamed in from the movie room. Deacon hummed under his breath, chest rumbling from it. "You're leaking for me, mate."

I felt the tip of my cock and my fingers came away wet.

"I'll give you a chance to come out, love."

Staying silent was hard. It wasn't the only thing hard. I stroked over my cock and nearly saw stars. Once he got his hands on me, I wouldn't last long.

We'll just have to do it again, my horny inner voice said, and I had to agree with it.

A growl filled the air and I smiled. His loud steps ate up the floor as he approached my hiding place. His form filled the small space.

"Mate," he clipped, taking both my hands and pulling them above my head. His body forced mine back until we hit the wall. "Mine."

"Deacon," I moaned when he used his other hand to run down my chest, stomach, and dick. He didn't stay there long, which had me whimpering in displeasure.

"Patience," he bit out, nipping at my jaw.

"I don't have any. I need you inside me. Need to feel you. Want you to fill me."

"Christ." His lips slammed down onto mine as he released and lifted me, hands to my ass. I wrapped my arms around his wide shoulders and my legs went around his waist.

The kiss was hungry and hot. Filled with a craving desire.

I rocked my hardness into him, moaning into his mouth.

Fingers slid down my crack, and he felt over my slicked hole. He groaned, picking me up a little to reach between us and line up his cock.

"Yes," I panted against his neck. "Please."

"Fucking hell, mate. You feel good, so fucking good." He grunted and clenched his jaw but held me still on his cock while he walked us out into the movie room.

I blinked at the light and moaned from his cock moving in me with each step. I kissed and bit at his neck and shoulder, making noises I'd never made before.

With ease, he took me off his cock, had me stand and then turned me, forcing my upper body down over the couch edge.

I arched, crying out when he thrust back into me. "Deacon," I breathed.

His fingers dug into my hips. He slipped back out and bucked in.

"Jesus," he groaned, snapping his hips back and forth. "Look at your hole taking my cock. Fucking perfect. Mine. So tight. I'll fill it, mate, and later I'll fuck your throat so you're full of my cum from both ends."

I mewed, sobbed, and whimpered. His words and the pleasure he built, overwhelmed me.

"Yes, yes, yes," I chanted.

I wanted that. No, I needed that. I wanted to be full of him all the fucking time.

"Come on, love. Come from my cock in you."

He adjusted his thrusts and hit my prostate over and over. Slamming my eyes closed, I moaned loudly as I spilled onto the floor.

"Fuck," Deacon growled low as he pushed in, pumping his cum inside me.

A tired, sedated laugh escaped me.

When Deacon pulled out, some of his cum leaked, until his thumb pressed against my hole and he forced it back in. A dirty moan escaped. I liked that he didn't want me to lose any of it. Him.

He helped me stand, turning me in his arms on shaky legs.

Smiling, I ran my hands up his chest. "We'd better clean up before you make good on your promise."

His brow arched. "Promise?"

I kissed and bit his neck. "To fuck my throat and fill me from both ends."

His gaze darkened once again. "You really want that?"

"Ah, yes." *Duh.* Wasn't it obvious I couldn't get enough of this man?

His grin was sinful. "Then let's clean in here and get you ready."

DEACON

"Y ou told me people didn't like being stared at. They could think it's creepy," Riker said from where he sat beside me at the table. A table I moved into the kitchen where I now did my work at the computer since my mate liked cooking and spent a lot of time in here.

"This is different," I told him absently, without looking away from Rio.

"Nope. You're looking creepy doing it."

Sighing, I stared at my brother. "Why aren't you still in the office with Nox?"

He shrugged. "Nox took off early, so I did."

"Why did Nox take off early?" He hadn't mentioned anything to me, and Nox usually went from the offices to home.

"I don't know."

Weird.

Did I need to call him?

"You're staring again," Riker commented.

"Riker," Rio called. "Leave your brother alone. He's allowed to stare at me. I like him staring at me. Now, if he stares at anyone else, you let me know." There was a jealous edge to his tone, and I fucking loved it.

I loved him.

Yet I hadn't told him, and we'd been together now for a few months.

Riker cackled. "You got it." He glanced back to me. "I'd totally tell on you to Rio."

Snorting, I palmed his face and shoved him back. "Where's the loyalty?" Not that it bothered me. I was glad my brother looked out for Rio.

"Your mate got Ruth and Grey to stay in town longer because she wants to get to know him. But most importantly, your mate cooks better than any of us. I'm not messing that up."

At least he was honest.

But my mate did cook like a seasoned chef, and he enjoyed trying out different recipes he'd learned in class.

"I can't say I blame you, Riker."

Rio winked before he put a tray into the oven and set the timer. He straightened, but then leaned over the counter, resting his chin on his hands.

Riker suddenly stood with a pained groan. "I know that look. You guys *always* get that look. I'm going for a run. Don't forget about my treats, though!"

Grunting, I heard him leave as I pushed my chair back to stand.

I drew in the scent around me, tasting my mate's desire as my cock thickened for him.

Christ, I could easily please my mate all day if he wanted. I'd never tire from watching him, scenting him, and taking him. I could listen to him talk for hours and hours.

He'd quelled my hard need for blood, and my bear didn't push at me as much to hunt and kill. I still enjoyed my jobs. Killing was fun, but I no longer hungered for it every day.

My mate had settled us.

He needed to know how much I loved him... and I'd tell him as soon as I fucked him.

Dropping to my knees behind him, I pulled down his pants and licked over his hole. He let out a breathy moan, pushing back on my face. I grabbed his hips and shoved my tongue inside him, and closed my eyes, heady over his smell and taste.

"Fuck, Deacon, yes." His back arched like a cat's, and he pushed back again.

I slipped a finger in and curled it. He clawed at the counter, moaning.

I fucking loved seeing him lost to the pleasure. To me.

Putting in another finger, I stretched him, licking around them.

"Deacon," Rio groaned. He slid the oil my way. I stood and pulled my fingers free to unbutton and zip down my pants. I dragged my aching cock free and then took up the liquid.

Undoing the cap, I poured some over Rio's crack and then into my palm to rub it over my length. I sucked in a sharp breath when Rio blindly pushed back into me, somehow managing to hit the right spot for my tip to breach his slicked-up hole, sucking it in.

"Fuck, love," I clipped.

"*Yes*. Yes!" he cried when I grabbed his waist and thrust further in.

A content hum dropped from my chest as his tightness enveloped around me. I could live inside him, his warmth choking my cock all the fucking time. His body was made for me.

I ran my hands up and over his back, slamming in and out of him, making him gasp and moan. Leaning over him, I licked and nipped at his shoulder.

"Please, harder, more. Deacon."

Reaching under him, I wrapped one arm around his waist and with the other, I fisted his cock. He let out a cry of desire as I held him still and my cock hammered into him.

"So good," I said. "My mate, my love, so fucking good. Want to be in you all the time."

"Yes, God, yes."

His walls squeezed around my cock as his dick erupted over my hand and the floor. I rested my forehead to his back and sucked in a deep breath. Having the scent of his cum in my senses tipped me over the edge, and I groaned long and low into his skin while I filled his ass.

Breathing heavily, I gently rocked the last of my seed into him as I straightened.

I stepped back, my spent dick falling free, relishing the sight of my cum leaking from him.

Rio let out a light laugh. "We'll have to clean this place and air it out or your brothers will kill us."

Helping him stand, I quickly stuffed my cock back in my pants and did them up. Rio turned and I picked my mate up. He clung to me like a koala and placed his head on my shoulder.

"I'll come back down and do it soon," I told him. "Let's get you in the shower."

He hummed and kissed my shoulder. "Shower sounds good. Besides, you have to wash all this oil off me."

Chuckling, I admitted, "I don't mind that task at all, love."

He patted my back. "Good." A gasp escaped him when an alarm went off. He pushed at my shoulders, and I let him down to run back over to the oven. He pulled out a tray of cookies and lay them on top of the oven.

"Riker would have my balls if I forgot—"

"He'd never have your balls," I stated gruffly.

Rio rolled his eyes, but said with a laugh, "You know what I mean. Thankfully, we were still here." Completely naked, he moved them one by one onto a cooling rack with my cum running down his legs. He couldn't be more perfect for me. I heard him lick his lips before saying, "I want to try these orange and chocolate muffins next. There's also that slow-cooked beef stew I saw the other day. Now I'm getting hungry smelling these. I think after our shower we can—"

"I love you," I blurted.

He stilled.

My ears rang from how hard and fast my heart was going. Even my bear tensed inside me a little, waiting for our mate's reaction.

Was it too soon?

We were committed. There was no going back for either of us, but still, saying those words meant a lot.

"Sorry?" he whispered.

Clearing my throat, I said again. "I love you."

He placed the spatula down and turned. His eyes glistened. "You do?"

"Yes, love. You're my fated, my lover, my friend, my jewel, and soul, breath, and heart. Everything. You've calmed and claimed me in all ways. I just needed you to hear those words. I love you, Rio, and I'll always love you."

Say it back. Please.

His bottom lip trembled, and he sniffed, wiping at his face.

A strangled laugh dropped from his mouth.

My gut clenched.

"You pick now to tell me. Is it because I'm oily naked with your cum in me?"

Huffing, I smirked. "Maybe."

His expression turned serious. "Deacon, I love you with my whole being too."

A shaky breath escaped. "Come here," I ordered.

He ran and jumped into my arms. I curled him in tightly, just as tight as he hugged me to him. I loved having him in my arms.

Into my shoulder, he said, "You've been the best thing

that happened to me. I know we have *many* more years together, but I hope each day goes slowly because it'll never be enough with you." He peppered kisses over my neck, chin, and finally lips, which turned into a claiming of its own. His tongue tangled with mine. I sucked on it, swirling ours together, and he rolled his cock against my stomach.

I couldn't get enough. I never would.

"Need you. Want to feel you in me again," he whimpered against me, rocking again.

I reached between us, undid the zipper, and pulled out my hard cock. And as I walked us to the bedroom and shower, I slipped back inside my mate to give him what he wanted.

RIO

LATER THAT NIGHT, I lay half on Deacon in bed and lifted my head to rest my chin on his chest. "Say it again?" I asked with a goofy smile on my lips.

He loved me.

I loved him.

Nothing could make me happier. I was warm on the inside and out.

If I had to thank Santiago for something, it would be for his illegal activities that drew Deacon's attention, else we wouldn't have met.

I wouldn't be in a bed with the man I was completely devoted to.

That thought shot a stream of fear into my veins, but I reminded myself of where I was.

Of whom I was lying on, and the fear vanished.

Deacon grinned, kissing the tip of my nose. "I love you—" A knock sounded on our door. Deacon called out, "Nox?"

His brother opened the door a little and stuck his head through. "Can I speak with your mate?"

"Me?" Shock had me sitting up, which meant the blanket fell from my shoulders to my lap.

Deacon picked it up and shoved it over my head. "Yes. Give him time," he ordered roughly, while I laughed and then shoved at the sheet after hearing the door close again.

"You're an idiot," I told him, slipping from the bed to get dressed.

"But an idiot you love."

Pausing, I stared down at him, lying back with his hands behind his head, and swooned.

I fucking *swooned*.

"You're right. I do love my idiot."

"Go see what my brother wants so you get back here quicker."

Winking, I made my way out of the bedroom, fully dressed, and found Nox pacing.

"What's—"

"Come with me," he said, and added tersely, "please."

Nodding, I followed him down the stairs and out toward the back of the house where his home offices were.

He opened the door, stepped back, and nodded me in while looking back down the halls.

I stepped into the room and halted.

What. The. Fuck?

Staring dumbfoundingly at the couch, I asked, "Nox, did you kidnap my professor?"

PROTECTED

BY THE BEAR SHIFTER

ACKNOWLEDGMENTS

To my readers who will pick up anything I write, thank you for sticking with me.

You probably know by now, 2023 was the hardest year I've had to date. Being diagnosed with breast cancer, the passing of my mother, and going through treatment.

I'm now hoping to get back on track with new and old characters, so keep an eye out these coming years.

To my new readers, thank you for giving Deacon and Rio a chance, I hope it paid off, and you're looking forward to Nox and Riker's stories soon!

ALSO BY L ROSE

The Hidden Kingdom Trilogy
(polyamorous fantasy romance)

A Torn Paige

A Lost Paige

A Final Paige

Infinite Bond

(m/m/m/m fantasy standalone)

Within the Darkness

(m/f/m/m fantasy standalone)

Titles under Lila Rose

Hawks MC: Ballarat Charter

Holding Out (Free)

Outplayed (standalone related to the Hawks MC)

Climbing Out

Finding Out (novella)

Black Out

No Way Out

Coming Out (m/m novella)

Out to Find Freedom (standalone related to the Hawks MC)

Hawks MC: Caroline Springs Charter

The Secret's Out

Hiding Out

Down and Out

Living Without

Walkout (novella)

Hear Me Out (m/m)

Break Out (novella)

Fallout

Out of the Blue (standalone related to the Hawks MC: m/m/m)

Out Gamed (standalone related to the Hawks MC: novella)

Hawks MC: Next Generation

Coyote

Ruin (m/m)

Texas

Polished P & P Series (m/m romance)

Wreck Me Forever

Never a Saint

Working Out West

Diamond MC

Country

State (novella)

Death

Romantic Comedies

Making Changes

Making Sense

***

Fumbled Love

Bumbled Love